# After Dinner Conversation

*Philosophy | Ethics Short Story Magazine*

December 2023

# After Dinner Conversation *Magazine* – December 2023

This magazine publishes fictional stories that explore ethical and philosophical questions in an informal manner. The purpose of these stories is to generate thoughtful discussion in an open and easily accessible manner.

Names, characters, businesses, organizations, places, events, and incidents are either the product of the author's imagination or are used fictitiously. Any resemblance to actual persons, living or dead, events, or locales is entirely coincidental. The magazine is published monthly in print and electronic format.

Vol. 4, No. 12

.

Copyright © 2023 After Dinner Conversation
Editor in Chief: *Kolby Granville*
Story Editor: *R.K.H. Ndong*
Acquisitions Editor: *Stephen Repsys*
Cover Design: *Shawn Winchester*
Design, layout, and discussion questions by After Dinner Conversation.

*https://www.afterdinnerconversation.com*

*After Dinner Conversation* believes humanity is improved by ethics and morals grounded in philosophical truth and that philosophical truth is discovered through intentional reflection and respectful debate. In order to facilitate that process, we have created a growing series of short stories across genres, a monthly magazine, and two podcasts. These accessible examples of abstract ethical and philosophical ideas are intended to draw out deeper discussions with friends, family, and students.

# Table Of Contents

\* \* \*

# From the Editor

Let's assume that for a given region, during a given time period, we could accurately rate the aggregate relative economic opportunity, social mobility, social safety nets, and political stability—a "hard work gets you the good life" rating.

However, time passes, and things change because of political instability, global manufacturing, and supply changes, or just geo-political luck. So, one group's "good life" rating for a period of time is 8/10, but their children's period is rated 5/10.

Do the parents have a duty to transfer their benefits to their offspring by paying for their education, technical training, housing down payments, or healthcare into adulthood? Or, can the parents say, "Look, I worked hard for this; I earned it. It's mine to keep and spend as I choose. Bummer you were born at the wrong time, but now you're an adult, so work hard, and you'll get something too, just maybe less than me."

Written correctly, this would make a great short story for our magazine. But my larger point is these questions are both infinite and common and could be written by anyone. The trick is learning to see the core issues in everyday situations.

By the way, in a survey we did, 64 percent said yes, parents in the situation above do owe a duty to their children, while 36 percent said they owe no duty at all...

Kolby Granville – Editor

# Being Wrong

## *Lise Halpern*

\* \* \*

"I am just not ready to see her, to sit down and eat a meal as if she has done nothing wrong." Katie spoke to her sister through the cell phone as she rushed to the school to pick up Tommy. "I can see her at Sharon's shower on Saturday, and I will be civil and polite and make nice small talk. I am just not up for a meal afterward or even a drink. I need to get home to the kids anyway."

And so it was. Donna traveled all the way back to Philadelphia to attend her niece Sharon's shower. She stayed in a hotel near her sister's house. She had dinner with an old school friend on Saturday night. She only saw her daughters at the shower.

At the shower, the girls each gave her kisses on the cheek and chatted happily about their lives. From the outside, it looked very normal. If asked if she was staying with one of the girls, Donna made their excuses. Eliza, Katie's youngest, was sick with croup. Marybeth was running a triathlon early Sunday morning. You know how busy it can be when you are young.

Donna knew full well the reality of why her daughters did not have time for her. It was written in the cold anger in Katie's eyes and stiff put-on-for-company smile. It was painted in the sadness and hurt around Marybeth's mouth as she told her about her trip to Maine with the current boyfriend. As far as they were concerned, it was all Donna's fault. She had smashed their perfect family.

Donna had met the girls' father, Ed, in a usual way, at a party at the home of a mutual friend. They dated in a usual way: movies, dinners out. Ed was devastatingly handsome, tall, slim, impeccably dressed. He had perfect manners and an easy smile. He laughed at her silly jokes and was kind and respectful to her parents. Everyone thought they were the perfect couple. Donna did too. Nobody was surprised when they got engaged, and that the wedding was a beautiful affair.

The first years of their marriage were beautiful too. They had a large fun circle of friends and went out every weekend. Ed was climbing the ladder at work, gaining responsibilities and salary. Eventually, according to plan and to no one's surprise, Donna got pregnant. She quit her job at the bank, and they bought a nice big stone house with a lawn and a swing set. She adored being a mother, adored Katie, adored building a beautiful home for them all to share.

They fell into a classic routine. Donna spent her days at home with Katie and, eventually, Marybeth too. She kept house, did the cooking, and made friends with other young mothers in the neighborhood. Ed worked long hours but was always happy to help with baths, read bedtime stories, and teach Katie to ride her tricycle on the weekend. There were fights, there were illnesses, there were bad days, and roof leaks, but overall, Donna loved her life.

Donna loved the big stone house. She loved her community of neighborhood mothers. She loved being the wife of an executive, buying nice clothing, hiring a decorator to help her build the most beautiful living room on the block. Mostly, she loved being a mom. She ran the PTO silent auction, provided snacks at every soccer game, and happily drove to every dance competition and track meet, no matter how far away from home.

Like a frog in a cold pot on a hot fire, Donna didn't notice at first when things started to get harder. Ed had always been super neat and organized. He saw mess as a personal affront, and he came to see it as Donna's responsibility to create a peaceful house where he could relax after work. He wanted clean, calm, and quiet to come home to, and that was Donna's job to provide. Donna did her best; she appreciated that he worked hard to support them financially and deserved a restful home at the end of the day.

However, kids are unpredictable, somewhat untrainable, and as their schedules got more complicated and time-consuming, she was less perfect at keeping things neat and calm. Ed would come home to find a board game spread out and abandoned, the contents of a backpack splayed across the kitchen floor. He would pop a cork. Sweep things out of the way. Scream at the kids, scream at Donna. Outbursts outsized for the seriousness of the infraction.

One day stands out. Maybe a pivot point? It was a small thing that crystallized the bigger issue and the choices she was making. Ed came home from work and tripped over Katie's soccer cleats as he walked in the door. He glared at Donna, picked up the cleats, walked outside, and threw them in the trash bin. "Dammit, Donna, the kids have to learn. If they treat their stuff like trash, then I am going to throw it in the trash. Don't you dare fish them out for her. Let her go to practice without cleats."

Donna had fished them out the next morning as soon as Ed left for work and before Katie left for school. She told Katie that her dad had thrown the shoes out, and now, she would have to wear "trash cleats" to practice. Katie scowled her displeasure. Donna made Katie wear the trash cleats for the entire week of practice, but took her for a new pair before the next game. Donna did not tell Ed; he did not have to know. Maybe this first subterfuge was where her marriage went wrong?

It turns out Ed did not have to know about a lot of things. Donna made it her mission to keep the girls out of range of his anger. She cleaned their rooms, hung up their dropped clothing. Ed never knew about Marybeth's detention for cutting class in high school or that Katie was caught smoking cigarettes behind the cafeteria. Donna alone cleaned up their messes; she soothed their hurt feelings and calmed their tantrums. Ed helped celebrate the soccer wins, the good report cards, the dance solos, and the college acceptances. He always bought the ice cream, the flower bouquets, and the celebration dinner.

Even on bad days, nothing made Donna happier than being Mom. She loved the long drives to tournaments, sitting outside endless Nutcracker rehearsals, chaperoning the school dance. It gave her those moments when her girls shared their innermost thoughts. The other moms became dear friends. They compared notes, complained about bad teachers, and the parents who drove the wrong way through the pick-up lane. As the children got older and needed less time, these friendships spread to lunches, tennis matches, golf lessons, and shopping trips into the city. Dealing with Ed's somewhat unrealistic demands was a small price to pay for living this magical life. She had successful, beautiful daughters, a beautiful home, and solid friendships.

Outside of the kids' commitments Donna and Ed spent less and less time together. Even more so as the girls graduated high school and moved on to college. Ed joined two fantasy football leagues, a weekly poker game, and had a regular tee time at the golf club. They went out on Saturday nights with friends and occasionally shared dinner at home during the week. They still shared a bedroom, but rarely went to bed at the same time.

Shortly after Marybeth left for college Ed had been asked to take over as the General Manager of the company's facility in Dallas. He bought a condo and came home to Pennsylvania every other weekend. Then he joined a golf club and a poker game in Dallas and started coming back every third weekend. When winter hit, and the weather was so much warmer in Texas, he started coming home only occasionally. He never invited Donna to join him in Dallas.

Donna built a bigger life for herself, living mostly alone in the big stone house in Pennsylvania. She layered on a part-time job at a boutique she loved downtown. She started taking a ceramics class. She went on trips with her girlfriends, a week to warm up in the Caribbean in January, and an annual golf trip to Hilton Head in March to kick off the season.

Donna's girls still came first, and she would drop anything

to be available to her now grown daughters. She skipped the club tournament one year to watch her first grandson, Tommy, while Katie and her husband stayed for a long weekend at a Vermont country inn. Donna knew how hard it was raising kids; they probably needed the break. Marybeth came home for a while after her breakup with her college boyfriend. Donna was thrilled that she seemed to find great comfort in her childhood bedroom, Mom cooked meals and laundry service. Donna helped her move into her new apartment a few months later, dragging boxes into the elevator just like the day they moved her into her first college dorm room.

Donna had never been that involved with the church, it was not her social set, but she did attend at least one Sunday a month. One Sunday, she saw the sign for the after-school tutoring program and was intrigued. This was something she could do; certainly, she had a lot of experience helping with homework. She signed up. The group met in the community room every Wednesday, and any school kid could stop by for help. One day she helped with a high school English paper, and the next week it was elementary school math. She loved it; it made her wistful for the days of helping the girls with homework.

One afternoon she was walking down the hall to the community room, reading a text from Katie. She was not paying attention, tripped over the toolbox in the hall, and splayed face-first on the floor. Chris, the man at the top of the ladder, scrambled down to help her, apologizing profusely for the toolbox on the floor. She apologized right back, saying it was her fault for walking while texting. They kept escalating the apologies until they both just started laughing.

Chris was a carpenter, working on some repairs for the church. It was a private job he did at a low rate after his day working for a developer building houses on what had until recently been a cornfield. He said it helped him balance his karma. During the day, he displaced cornfields with townhouses, cutting down trees and reducing open space. After work, he helped the church with much needed repairs.

Donna instantly liked him. He was not traditionally handsome. He had lost his hair young and broken his nose in a worksite accident. His body was lean and strong, but his hands were rough and scarred from daily labor. His smile, however, was warm, and he looked her in the eye when she spoke and really listened to her words. She stopped to chat with him most days when she was tutoring. He had a strong curiosity about the world and about Donna. They talked about the students she tutored, about her golf game, and her daughters. He said he had been married and had a son and an ex-wife, both living in California. After his divorce, he took this job with Caruso Brothers Construction and now moved every one or two years to supervise construction of their next development and find a side job to balance that karma.

To this day Donna is not quite sure how it happened, how their relationship grew as the townhouses rose out of the cornfield. They found themselves talking at church, then going out to dinner, then sharing a bed. In a strange way, Donna did not think Ed would mind. Even when he came home to Pennsylvania, they slept in different bedrooms. Ed had a life in Dallas, and Donna realized she would not be surprised or disappointed if that life also included him sharing a bed with another woman. She knew this was a betrayal, but it felt like a soft one, an extension of all the other things they had come not to talk about.

Eventually, the townhouses were finished. Cars started appearing in driveways, people were moving in, and Chris was moving out. He was scheduled to head to North Carolina to build a 55+ development. Suddenly, her private relationship with Chris was crashing into her real out loud life, and she had a decision to make. Chris offered to leave Caruso Brothers and stay in Pennsylvania. He offered to leave, with a broken heart, and let her continue her life as if he had never existed. He also invited her to come to North Carolina. Chris made it clear he wanted to be with her, but only if she wanted to be with him. She was the one in the marriage, and he understood that choosing him might be the wrong thing for Donna. It was her decision.

Donna knew this was a choice not between Chris and Ed, but a choice between Chris and the life she had been living—the lovely stone house, her friends, her golf club. She could not have both. Her friends were not close to Ed, some of them barely knew him, but she knew they would see her divorcing Ed and shacking up with her lover as an affront to their values. Sue Trachtman had divorced her husband a few years ago. She had moved into the city and was pretty much forgotten by her old circle. Donna met her for lunch once a year or so, chatting about grandchildren and the old times on the sidelines of the soccer field.

Donna knew what she wanted to do. She would miss her friends, the house, the boutique, the golf club, even the church, but she wanted to go to North Carolina with Chris. To live out in public with the man she had grown to love, and she knew with absolute certainty, loved her in return.

Donna told Ed on his next visit to Pennsylvania. It was a simple conversation at the kitchen table. She said those fateful words, "I want a divorce."

He asked, "Why get a divorce? Why not just go on living our lives? Sell the house if you want, move away, do whatever you want. But divorce is expensive and complicated. It's bad for the kids, bad for my career, bad for both of us. Just leave things as they are."

Donna said, "Because I have met someone else." Ed looked away, staring out the kitchen window. He frowned into her eyes and said, "You're not getting all the money." He went back to Dallas the next morning.

"How can you leave Dad for that nobody." That was Katie's first reaction when Donna shared her plan to divorce Ed and move to North Carolina with Chris.

"Dad will be so alone, and you are picking up and leaving all your friends and family for the sake of a fling?" Marybeth cried. "Thirty-one years, Mom, how can you just walk away from thirty-one years?"

The girls were right. Chris was a carpenter, not particularly well educated, debonair, or handsome. Ed was a division VP at a big electronics manufacturer. He was Ivy League, fit, well-dressed, still had all his hair. By any objective standard, she was stepping down the socioeconomic ladder. She was also walking away from a lifetime investment. Thirty-one years of building her picture-perfect life.

The girls were also wrong. Moving with Chris was not walking away from perfect; it was walking toward amazing. They did not know Chris, did not see his kindness, his gentle soul. They never saw how he made her laugh through the ordinary and held her hand through the ugly.

They had also never seen the truth of that thirty-one-year marriage. The girls did not realize that no one was being hurt by her decision to leave. Donna was happy, Ed was ambivalent, and the girls were perfectly fine. Donna realized she had been wrong to have kept everyone in the dark all those years. Even when they were grown, she had not let them see the truth. She had protected them, protected Ed, protected everyone from each other. She had known her girls would be upset, but she had been surprised at the level of anger and hurt. She knew what she had done was wrong, but Ed was the one wronged, not the girls. Ed did revel a bit in their fury at her; it was a bit of revenge that they were on "his side." He knew that hurt her.

Donna packed up the house and put it on the market. She packed up the girls' rooms, all their childhood mementos and outgrown clothing. Neither of them were taking her calls, so she rented them each a storage locker. Eventually, after she had moved to North Carolina, Katie relented a little. Donna called Tommy on his birthday, and Katie let them talk. Communications were restored, if only on a very logistical level.

Donna loved her daughters. Overall, they were kind, smart, caring, good people. However, somehow, as they had watched their father value her only for what she did for the house and family, measure her performance by his comfort, they began to do the same. She only allowed them to see her as caretaker, as fixer, as parent. They could not see her as a person. A person who could make mistakes, have regrets, love, and want to be loved.

Donna knew it was now too late to tell her daughters her

side of the story, to try to get them to see her life. They would have to reconsider so many fundamental feelings and memories, examine their own behavior in a different light. Nobody wants to rewrite the past, particularly their happy childhood. She didn't really want to burst that illusion anyway. Their happy adulthoods were shaped by their happy childhoods, and she wanted them to be happy.

Now, the only hope was a waiting game. Waiting for them to cool down and relent or maybe to experience enough friction in their own lives to give her a little grace. Waiting maybe for them to experience more of their father, now unprotected, and maybe consider a different narrative. Maybe one day, she would be invited for Thanksgiving dinner and maybe even invited to bring Chris.

Donna boarded the plane for Charlotte, pulling her small suitcase behind her through the jetway. Chris was meeting her at the airport. They would grab a pizza on the way home. He would show her the cabinets he had installed in the guest bath while she was away. They would sit on the patio and listen to the night. He would hold her hand, and she would tell him about the noisy kids next door in the hotel room, Sharon's lovely shower, and seeing her daughters.

* * *

# Discussion Questions

1. If you were Donna's friend, what advice would you have given her *before* she asked for a divorce? Would you have advised her to try and fix her marriage?

2. Should a divorce and a new relationship ever be combined, or should you divorce because you are unhappy and only later seek a new relationship? Why are the two so often related?

3. What (if anything) should Donna do about her children's anger toward her? Should she reach out to them? If so, what should she say? Should she risk altering their happy childhood memories by telling her perspective?

4. What rights should Donna have to their house, savings, and retirement, given that she rarely worked for money during their marriage and has no work history?

5. Whose fault is the failed marriage? To what extent was Donna obligated to tell her husband she was unhappy in their marriage? Would it matter if Ed was also unhappy and said nothing but simply decided to have affairs and stick it out? Do married couples deserve ongoing love or only ongoing mutual respect and support?

* * *

# The Children of Conscious Reunion

*M.C. Schmidt*

\* \* \*

It was nearly nine o'clock, and someone was knocking on Ana Marie's storm door. She laid her dishrag in the sink and walked into the living room with Banjo coming along behind her. As she approached the foyer, she saw the caller was a woman, elderly, older than Ana Marie by at least a decade. She was small, too, no threat at all. That was a relief, given the hour. "Yes?" Ana Marie called.

"You'll take me now, I hope," the woman said. "I saw your sign."

"My sign?" Ana Marie asked but realized the woman's meaning even before she'd finished the question. "Oh, yes! I can take you." She noted the bound accordion folder the woman cradled in her arms and felt a little thrill. She unlatched the door and pushed it open. "Welcome," she said. "Please, come in."

The woman stepped into the foyer, trailed by the

fragrance of orchids. "I've never had to do this before if you can believe it," she said. Her manner seemed curt, almost put-upon, as if Ana Marie had caused her a great hassle. "I wasn't sure how to find you other than by driving around and looking. I'm useless with the Internet, and they haven't delivered a Yellow Pages in years."

Ana Marie didn't say so, but she'd never done this before, either. She'd only received her certification three days earlier. When the packet arrived, she'd made an announcement on Facebook and affixed the decal to her front picture window: *Certified Notary Public.* She'd gotten no response until now. "Are you selling a car?" she asked, leading the woman through the living room. "What was your name? I'm Ana Marie."

"Regina," the woman said, "and, no, I'm not selling anything." At the far sound of her voice, Ana Marie turned to see Regina had come to a stop, trapped by Banjo, who was making a show of greeting her, sniffing her shoes and knees, his tail fanning wildly.

Ana Marie commanded him to heel in the tone that Gus had taught her. The dog turned and came to her, sitting and bouncing on his haunches to show that she had called him away from important business. To her guest, she asked, "Can I offer you something? Tea, maybe? Or water?"

"I'd prefer we get down to it," Regina said. She stepped into the dining room ahead of Ana Marie and laid her folder on the dining table's worn wooden top. "Is this good?"

"It's fine," Ana Marie said, showing a hint of pique. The woman was here on business, sure, but she was still a visitor in someone's home, and politeness was free. "I'll get my things."

\* \* \*

They sat with their chairs pushed close enough together that they could easily pass documents between them. With her new ink stamp and embosser and notary journal in front of her, Ana Marie felt like a student on the first day of school, sitting primly with fresh supplies. Banjo lay at their feet.

"I need to transfer the deed to my home," Regina said, removing a stack of papers from her accordion folder and handing them to Ana Marie. "It's paid off, of course. I own it outright."

Ana Marie removed the paperclip from the stack and laid the pages side by side in front of her. Three blank copies of a general warranty deed. She looked over each copy, saying nothing, reading each from top to bottom.

"Is there a problem?" Regina asked after several minutes had passed.

Ana Marie suspected there was. "Wouldn't you rather have a lawyer process this? A house is a significant asset."

"A lawyer won't be necessary," Regina said, her tone suggesting this had already been considered and her answer was final. "I'm the property owner. I am who I say I am." From her folder, she removed a driver's license and a social security card that were bound with a rubber band. She slapped them on the tabletop. Ana Marie glanced at the photo on the license and read the name: Regina Rea Mitchell. "It's my property, and it's my decision. Not my lawyer's and not my son's."

"You're granting the property to your son?" Ana Marie asked. "Would it be possible for him to join us?"

Regina snorted. "No," she said, "I am not signing over my home to my son. We aren't on speaking terms just now. The property is going to Father."

Ana Marie raised her head from the paperwork. She didn't want to be rude, but surely the woman wasn't serious. Or, if she was serious, she wasn't mentally well. "I'm sorry," she said as delicately as she could, "you're transferring the house to your father?"

"I don't mean my birth father, clearly. Daddy's been in Spring Grove since I was five. I'm granting the home to my spiritual father. The Messiah. Jackson Muehl, if you like. That's His terrestrial name in the kingdom of man."

"The... kingdom of man?"

"Yes, precisely," she said. "I want Father to take over the deed. That's my legal right, is it not?"

"It is," Ana Marie allowed.

"Then why aren't we moving forward?"

"It's just—before we even talk about what needs to happen with this paperwork, I have to make sure I understand the situation."

Regina lifted her chin as if she was dealing with someone whose station was beneath her. "I'm not particularly bothered if you understand the situation or not. Others' lack of understanding is a thing I've gotten used to."

"Yes," Ana Marie said, "but as a state authority, I'm going to need you to explain it to me." She felt a sense of imposter syndrome, calling herself an authority. Her inkpad had never been pressed. Her rubber stamp was pristine. Nevertheless, she opened her notary journal and positioned her pen to write on its first page. "So," she said, "explain it to me. Are you granting the property to the church as an institution or your pastor as an individual?"

"Father is a prophet," she said, "not a pastor. And He *is* the church. They're one and the same."

"Mm-hmm. And does the church have a name and a physical address?"

Regina seemed hesitant to name the group, but finally, she said, "We are the Children of Conscious Reunion. And, yes, we have a ranch. That's where I'll live after this deed is settled. Several of us have already done it."

Ana Marie was grateful the journal gave her somewhere to focus her eyes, something to do with her hand. "And do they have tax-exempt status under 501 (c) (3)?"

"I have no way of knowing that."

"That's something you'll want to know," Ana Marie said. "That's the first thing. Also, he'll need to be present to sign at the time of notarizing, and you'll need to bring a witness."

"Wait," Regina said, "are you saying I'll have to come back?"

"I'll need the grantee and a witness to be present. It's state law."

Regina smacked her fist on the table, causing Banjo to skitter out from under it. He circled behind Ana Marie's chair, where he stood like a sentry, alert and ready if called upon. Ana Marie began to scold her guest for her rudeness but stopped at the site of tears in her eyes. "Regina?" she asked.

"I can't!" she cried. "I can't bring Him here!" Without warning, her face had contorted from its previous sternness to a wide-eyed expression of panic.

"I'm sorry," Ana Marie said. She nearly reached to take the woman's hand but instead tightened her grip on her pen. "If he's done this with other... congregants, then he should know that he needs to be present."

"But it's a surprise! He doesn't know! I need this to be a surprise!" She hid her face in her tiny hands. "You don't understand," she repeated over and over into her tented palms.

"What don't I understand?" Ana Marie asked.

When Regina finally revealed her face, her cheeks and upper lip were slick and shiny. "We're coming into the final phase! That doesn't mean anything to you now, but it will. There's no hope for anyone outside of the ranch. I'd be living there already if my son hadn't involved himself. Do you want to know what he did to me? He kidnapped me from the worship hall with some goon, a so-called deprogrammer. He caused such a stink for Father that He banished me. That's a death sentence. That's eternal damnation." She grabbed the closest copy of the deed and waved it, crumpling it in her first. "This was a surprise for Him. This was to show Him my commitment, so He'll let me back in while there's still time. Now you say you won't help me. Now you're killing me all over again."

It was a ridiculous accusation. Ridiculous, but it worked to make Ana Marie doubt herself. The woman's stare was so pleading, so needful, that she felt embarrassed for them both. There was, of course, nothing in her training to prepare her for a situation like this. She wasn't a counselor or a caregiver; she was a stamp and a signature, a mental list of rules. She was a recent retiree who wanted to earn some extra cash and nothing more than that. It was agonizing for her to sit and say nothing, but she had nothing further to say.

Eventually, Regina blinked and looked away, freeing Ana Marie to do the same. The older woman lifted the top of the accordion folder, opening its mouth wide. She was peering into it, hiding her face, when she asked, "Do you understand why it's so important I get this done now, tonight?" Her voice was quiet and strained, like it took some effort to control it.

"Yes," Ana Marie said.

Regina withdrew a travel pack of tissues from the folder and carefully pulled one free. She blotted the corners of her eyes and both nostrils before hiding the tissue in her closed fist and returning her hands to the tabletop. "So, will you help me?"

"I'm sorry," Ana Marie said. "There's nothing I can do."

The older woman didn't respond immediately, just set about stacking the deeds and collecting her identification cards. Ana Marie watched as she banded all of this into the tidy bundles she'd arrived with and returned them to her folder. Once she'd secured the folder with its elastic band, she moved her eyes to Ana Marie's supplies, studying them for a moment before looking again at Ana Marie herself. "Is that true?" she asked. "Or are you lying because you don't want to help me?"

"It's true," Ana Marie said, holding her gaze.

Regina nodded. "Fine," she said and then abruptly rose from the table. Banjo yipped and jumped out of the way of her chair legs. Regina snatched up the folder and clutched it against her chest. "Fine," she said again and turned away from the table. Ana Marie remained seated long after she heard her storm door slam, listening to the clacking of Banjo's claws on the foyer tile, his confused dance, and interrogative whine.

* * *

"So," Gus asked, "was it true, or were you just trying to get rid of her?"

"No, it's true," Ana Marie said. "It's the law. I was glad when she left, though."

He laughed a big man's bellowing laugh and said, "I bet."

They were sitting side by side at a picnic table at the dog park, positioned the wrong way with their backs resting against the table's edge so they could watch Banjo and Betty, Gus's Newfoundland, playing in the fenced-in run. Banjo never looked more like an adorable mutt to Ana Marie than when he was running and roughhousing with his purebred buddy. For a while, they were silent, watching the dogs charge through an obstacle course again and again. Eventually, Gus said, "I just can't quit thinking about it. That's crazy, having a real-life cult member show up at your door."

"Ex-cult member," Ana Marie reminded him. "She got kicked out."

"Still, it's freaky."

"It really was. The funny thing is, you always hear how cultists sign over their assets to their leader, but I never even thought about how that would work practically. I mean, it's easy enough to transfer money, but what about IRAs and 401(k)s and properties? It turns out they do it through people like me. That's what *I* keep thinking about."

"Yup, freaky," Gus said again. A young woman walked in front of them then, led by a leashed terrier. She smiled, and they each nodded. Gus followed her with his eyes. When he turned back to Ana Marie and saw that she'd noticed, he gave her a devilish grin. "What were we talking about?"

"Cults," Ana Marie said, playfully bumping his big shoulder with her own.

"Sorry, yeah. I got distracted by something. You don't think she'll come back with the guy, do you? What was his name?"

"Jackson Muehl. I looked him up, and the group, but I

didn't get any hits. I found a bunch of pictures of men with that name, so one of them might have been him, but I don't know for sure."

"But if she brings him over with the witness, will you do it?"

"How could I?"

"Nah, I didn't figure you would. But three on one could be intimidating just the same. Do you want me to sleep over the next few nights just in case?"

Ana Marie rolled her eyes. "Why don't you go chase after that terrier woman if you're looking for a sleepover?"

"An old codger like me? I'm apt to give myself a heart attack, just trying to catch up to her to ask her for a date. That's not what I was talking about anyway."

"I know," Ana Marie assured him. It wasn't unheard of for them to have the occasional sleepover, but those were strictly needs-based transactions, the oil change and tire rotation of two happy, single, older people who loved but were not attracted to one another. She wasn't going to fall into his arms and pull him into her bed just because she was afraid of some cult leader. "Thank you, Gus, but I don't think she'll come back. And if she does, I have Banjo."

"That you do. If they show up, though, don't let them in. And call me. I'll come right over." Ana Marie squeezed his knee, and they went back to watching the dogs, who were taking a break from their frenetic play, each drawing greedy laps from the doggie drinking fountain. "Where was her house, anyway?" Gus asked.

"Hmm?"

"The old lady. Where was the house she was trying to give

up?"

"Oh, I don't remember. Uptown somewhere, I think. I'm not sure."

"Well, dang. I might have liked to drive past it, just for curiosity's sake."

"Yeah," she agreed, looking down at her hands, "it's too bad."

\* \* \*

Ana Marie had imagined the house would be nicer. There'd been something almost regal in Regina's attitude before her meltdown. It was a snobbishness, if Ana Marie was being honest, that had given the impression Regina was from the upper crust. As it turned out, the house was just a modest ranch, no bigger than her own. From where she was parked, she could see it wasn't even the biggest on the block.

She wasn't sure why she'd lied to Gus. She'd had no good reason. It hadn't even occurred to her to drive over for a peek at the house until the very moment he'd asked about it. She'd logged Regina's address in her notary journal, of course, not that she needed to look it up. It felt deceitful driving there straight from the dog park, but as soon as he brought it up, she knew it was just what she would do.

The house was on the opposite side of town from Ana Marie's, the east end near the Catholic high school and the old hospital building. From the similarity in design to her own home, she suspected this neighborhood had been built in the early sixties, just as hers had been. Regina even had the same worn green turf glued to her porch that Ana Marie had repeatedly tried and failed to scrape and pry off her own.

When they'd first arrived, Banjo had been ecstatic,

pushing his nose against the backseat windows and snorting, taking in all he could see of that unfamiliar street. He'd whined curiously when Ana Marie made no move to get out of the car and eventually seemed to accept this wasn't to be the adventure he'd assumed. He'd then lain down across the backseat, keeping his disappointment to himself like the stoic trooper she knew him to be.

They sat that way for some time—engine off; Banjo sleeping; Ana Marie gazing at the fluttering leaves of the oak tree in the yard beside Regina's, the occasional passing car. She mostly avoided staring at the house itself.

She'd come with no plan, but what she really wanted, she now realized, was to see Regina herself. Maybe for reassurance that she was okay after the state she'd left in. Maybe for reasons less high-minded than that, she wasn't sure. Curiosity or some similarly vulgar motive. It occurred to Ana Marie she wasn't all that different from Regina. She'd never had a child, thank God, so she didn't know how it felt to be estranged from a son. Still, she knew well what it was like to be an independent woman of a certain age. She'd always had the good sense to maintain friendships with solid people who would be there for her if she needed them. Even now, she had Banjo and Gus and a few others who would have her back. Where would she be if she were really, truly on her own? Might she find herself so lonely that she'd be taken in by a charismatic man who offered love and family if you'd only listen to his mumbo jumbo? Maybe. It really was possible. Ana Marie had seen documentaries. She knew that anyone could fall into a group like that under the right circumstances. So, had she come to Regina's house to check up on her? Or, had she arrived secretly hoping to see something strange—the woman dead on her lawn from drinking a poisoned children's drink or gesticulating wildly in her front window, aggressively praying like some lunatic—to make Ana Marie feel better about her own life choices? It was troubling not knowing for sure.

From the corner of her eye, she became aware of movement at Regina's house. She looked to see that the front door was now open, and a man was moving down the driveway toward her. He was stocky and middle-aged. He looked angry and was coming quickly. "Oh, hell," Regina said as she scooted up from her slouch in the driver's seat. She was fumbling with the ignition and pedals—how that blasted machine worked, she suddenly couldn't recall for the life of her—when the man set upon her car, yelling and slamming his hand on her window. The car was filled with the thump of his palm and the tack of the ring on his finger.

Banjo awoke and was immediately on his feet on the backseat, snarling at the man, scratching at the back window, and barking thunderous warnings. The man jumped back, startled by the dog's sudden appearance. It took several commands for Ana Marie to silence Banjo, and even then, she could hear him wheezing and whining behind her.

The man stood in the middle of the street, now recording her with the camera on his phone. He was wide-eyed as if it had been Ana Marie who had tried to attack him and not the other way around. "You all are bringing dogs now?" he called. Ana Marie didn't register his words. She only turned her face away from him and fumbled in her attempt to get the car started and into drive. He came nearer to her window again, imposing if not openly aggressive. "Hey," he said, "they're sending you out here with dogs now to scare us?"

"What?" Ana Marie asked, confused and embarrassed and a little frightened. "No. Go away." Her wits were returning to her, and she succeeded in starting the car.

"Wait, no!" the man called. "I want to talk to you." When she made no reply, he said, "You tell Father she isn't here anymore. And he isn't going to find her, either. Tell him if he agrees to back off and stop sending you all out here, he won't have any more trouble from me. You tell him her son says it's over; enough is enough."

Regina's son. Of course, he was.

"I'm not one of them," Ana Marie said, finally turning to look at him.

He was staring at her with his mouth slack. "Bull," he said.

"I'm just—I'm a friend of your mom's. I only wanted to check on her."

"A friend of Mom's from where?"

What could she say? She didn't know a thing about this woman, except that she'd been in a cult. She could be honest, she supposed, tell him what his mother had tried to get her to do behind his back. Or, she could have said nothing, just driven away. "Church," she tried. "Her old church from before."

For the first time since he'd rushed at her, the man's face relaxed into an expression that approached civility. "You're from St. Matthews?"

Ana Marie nodded. "Yes. Will you please stop filming me?"

He lowered his phone but didn't put it away. "What's with the dog?"

"He's just my dog. You scared him." The man didn't

apologize, but he seemed to accept this answer. He nodded and shut down his camera and slid the phone into the pocket of his jeans. "Thank you," she said.

"Hey, can you, like, crack your window or something so I don't have to yell at you?"

That wouldn't be wise, given his behavior. Gus would tell her not to, and she would advise the same thing to him if the roles were reversed. "My dog is well-trained," she called, "but he'll attack if he sees I'm in any danger."

"You won't be," the man said, taking a step back and raising his hands in surrender. "You aren't. It was—I thought you were somebody else."

Ana Marie glanced back at Banjo, who nosed past the strap of her seatbelt to rest his head on her shoulder. She wiped her hand gratefully down his face and then powered the window open a few inches.

"Good looking animal," the man said, "when it's not baring its teeth. My name's Calvin."

"Betty," Ana Marie said.

"Nice to meet you, Betty. I didn't mean to scare you by storming out here, but I've been getting nothing but grief from that lot Mom was mixed up with ever since I got her out of there. I assume you know about all that. That's why you came out?"

"I don't know much," Ana Marie said. "Only that she found a new church, and I never saw her again. There's been some talk, so I thought I'd pop over to check on her."

Calvin shook his head and stared at the ground. "I've got to say, I'm real embarrassed that it got back to you all over there at St. Matts. I don't know what you've heard, but to me this group isn't much of a church at all."

"How do you mean?" she asked, creasing her brow as if confused.

The man who had moments before been slamming his hand against her window now seemed pensive, almost shy. "Ah, well, I mean, Mom and I never had the best relationship, but we were fine until she got caught up with those people. I'd come over to see her, and it was like talking to a different person, like she was brainwashed or something, going on and on about the phases of Revelations and heaven being a planet in some other galaxy, and I don't know what all."

"Goodness," Ana Marie said. It was the correct thing, she thought, for a churchgoer to say. "But you said you got her out of it?"

"Yeah, I don't want to get too much into that with you, Betty, but we had to force them to let her go. It took some doing too. And ever since then, they've been harassing us: stealing Mom's trash from the curb here, following me from my house to work, all kinds of crazy stuff. I don't even know what they're trying to achieve with all that except to scare me away from talking bad about them. But, I mean, to who? Who would care what I had to say? Coo-coo birds, every one of them."

"That's really upsetting," Ana Marie said.

"It is definitely that. But, look," he said, tapping the chrome beneath the car window with his fingertips, "I know you came out here to see her, but Mom isn't at home right now. She won't be available for at least a few days."

"She's okay, I hope."

"Well, we'll see. We had a bit of a situation here last night. She ended up getting checked into the hospital."

The blood drained from Ana Marie's face. "The church?"

she asked.

"Oh, no, they didn't do anything to her. Well, I mean, not directly. She ended up calling me late, all in a panic. It turns out she tried to do something yesterday to get back in their good graces. I'd rather not say what. When she couldn't pull it off, she thought the right thing to do was to call and get me out of bed, cursing me out and blaming it on me, even though I didn't know what in the heck she was talking about. I ended up driving over here, and, long story short, she worked herself up so much that she wound up at the hospital."

"That's—that's terrible," Ana Marie said. "Could I visit her there?" She wasn't sure if she was asking as Betty or as herself.

"No, ma'am, I'm afraid not," Calvin said. "It's not that kind of hospital. And, truth be told, whenever she gets out, it might be time to think about a care home. She hasn't been filling me with confidence lately that she's in good shape to look after herself."

Ana Marie thought of that tiny, imposing woman who'd shown up at her door. Fit to drive herself, search for and find a random notary, and obtain the documents needed to legally set her admittedly ill-conceived plan in motion. She might need some help, sure, maybe even that brief stay at a hospital. But a long-term care home? She didn't buy it. It was the fate she had always most dreaded for herself, ending up in a facility like that. It was scarier even than falling in her home and breaking a hip and not being found in time to be saved.

"Are you all right, Betty?"

She was staring past him at Regina's porch, absently scratching Banjo's head. "Yes," she said, coldly. "Just a little sad. I'll let you go now."

"Do you want me to take down your number so I can let you know when she's settled somewhere?"

"That won't be necessary." She powered up the window, closing herself off from him, and then drove away. Calvin was still standing in the street when she checked her rearview mirror before turning onto the main road.

It was a short drive from Regina's house to Ana Marie's, less than ten minutes if she didn't get stopped by the train that seemed to run constantly into and out of the steel mill. As she drove, she imagined various ways she might help the woman—fanciful things like busting her out of the hospital and bringing her home to live with Banjo and herself or bending the law by notarizing her deed to at least give her a chance to end up in the prison of her own choosing. It wouldn't last, she knew. In the end, she would do nothing. How could she? It wasn't her problem to solve. She would get home from this drive and walk into her house, and her own life would resume. From time to time, she would probably think of Regina, and she hoped those moments would remind her to be grateful for Banjo and Gus and those few others who kept her tethered to the world. Eventually, Regina would just be the central character in a story Ana Marie would sometimes tell, one whose title might be "You'll Never Believe the Crazy Thing That Happened to Me Once." For the moment, though, she imagined herself a savior: turning around and confronting the son, explaining to him that by imposing his will on her and sending her to a care home, he was being as manipulative as the cult leader, convincing him to take Regina into his own home for the few good years she had left. At Christmas, she would receive an unexpected card from Regina, thanking her for bringing them back together. Ana

Marie would continue to receive those cards, one per year, until the year when a card didn't come, and she would know the woman had completed a life that ended happily.

Ahead of her, cars slowed. The lights were flashing on either side of the railroad crossing, and the barrier arm was lowering. Ana Marie slowed to a stop. She met Banjo's eye in the rearview and said, "We're going to be stuck out here for a while." Banjo yawned at her and smiled and resumed watching the curiosities unfolding around him, unburdened by worries, unable to imagine a world in which he was not loved.

* * *

# Discussion Questions

1. Ana Marie was prevented from notarizing the deed because of a technicality. If that technicality had not existed, should she have notarized the deed and allowed the house transfer? Should she have tried to talk Regina out of the transfer?
2. Are there certain traits a person has that are more likely to fall in with a cult? What would you say to a friend you believed had fallen in with a cult? What traits would the group have to show for you to know it's a cult?
3. Did Regina's son have a right to take her away from her church/cult without her permission? Does Regina have the right to change (or ruin) her life in whatever way she sees fit, so long as it doesn't hurt anyone else?
4. What is the difference between selling your house to pay for a care facility in your old age and giving your house to a church/cult to take care of you in your old age?
5. If joining a church/cult brought your own mother a genuine sense of belonging and happiness, would you support her decision?

* * *

# The Pill

## *Thea Swanson*

* * *

Marlee stopped taking the pill when she was fifty-two. She had been bleeding each month—albeit hardly and close to tar—so she figured she was fertile, sort of, that something would attach itself to her uterine lining even if not completely thriving. She thought herself to be a woman who could have babies easily and forever if she didn't take measures. She had had two, and each one had been planned insofar as the condom was removed that month for that purpose, and one spermatozoon had made contact both times on the first try, digging their pushy little heads into her waiting eggs so that the following month, the test read positive. At her recent mandatory checkup with her new primary doctor, Marlee went over the facts of her body quickly to get the meeting over with, and when mentioning the pill and then receiving the pause, Marlee said, "I'm still bleeding," and was told, "That's because you're taking the pill," and Marlee said, "Oh."

Marlee was not stupid. She had earned a master's degree

in business administration and had applied decades of fundraising expertise in development offices in Seattle. Moreover, she acquired great wisdom, leading and sometimes winning household wars for close to thirty years. The correct day to stop the pill was not on her mind. When Marlee was thirty-eight, she learned she was anemic from bleeding too much, and the pill lightened the flow. Who knew the reason she had pressed her cheek to the kitchen counter was not from cooking yet another meal but from oxygen deficiency? The pill allowed her to do many, many tasks.

Her new doctor typed Marlee's spoken data in her digital record.

"I'll stop then," Marlee said.

"Your hormone replacement therapy could be pills—the most common, but there are patches and creams too." The doctor peered at the screen. "You don't have high blood pressure or any—"

"Can't I just stop taking the pill?"

The doctor regrouped. "You could, but you may find the sudden change difficult. You might find the hot flashes and night sweats unbearable."

"I've been having night sweats for years."

"Then you're probably already perimenopausal. You could try it and see how it goes." The doctor tapped the keyboard. "If you suffer too much, we can look at your HRT options." The doctor stopped typing and looked straight at Marlee, causing her to straighten her sitting posture. "After one full year without a period, you will not need protection from pregnancy. Use something else in the meantime."

Marlee finished her pill pack, and all blood ceased. Emotionally, she was exactly the same. It was clear she had already gone through menopause. A few years back, she'd wake at two a.m., sweat pooling around her torso, and she didn't think of menopause. As far as she knew, the cessation of menstruation was the turning point. She had never talked about these things with her mother or any woman, had not looked them up. If her OB/GYN, whom she avoided regularly, ever mentioned menopause, she couldn't remember.

Marlee's sex drive also ceased the day she stopped the pill. During the previous decade, her libido had been a thing she'd conjure when necessary or if nudged by the touch of her husband. Occasionally, she'd view an image that would titillate, causing warmth to rush to the vulva, and if completely alone, which was close to never, she'd close the bedroom door and indulge in two minutes of lushness, then grab her jeans she had stepped out of and go on with her day. Sex, to her, had been, for quite some time, an interruption of things that mattered. There were things she wanted to do in any given twenty-four-hour period, and boosting her husband's self-confidence, which is what sex had become for the past ten years, was not on her list, though it always seemed to make its way there. Yes, her life had been one of tending to others. Five seconds of orgasm—and the two hours of building up his ego beforehand with coffee or beer and attentive listening—robbed her of a beautiful morning run or three absorbing chapters before sleep.

Without the pill, her conjuring resulted in nothing. No matter the fantasy or body part, she could not be moved, save for a distant, focused, brief rise and fall. And if it was just her body that was of concern, she would have celebrated with a bath, a candle, and Pinot Gris—a bath that was not to prepare oneself for the pleasure of another but simply because it felt good to Marlee. A bath from beginning to end with only Marlee in mind. No shaving and staying in the water till sleep. But there was this other body that used hers for its purposes. Love and affection, sure, but coming at her were also body parts, and she was feeling like an apparatus now more than ever. Hostility brewed within her, surfacing in private moments on her lips and brow. How many years must a woman be a tool for all to use? And when the day would come that she wasn't of use, she was sure to shuffle in her pastel pants through the halls of a nursing home, tossed away.

With menopause came a knowing. Commercials advertising male supplements she now viewed with pinpointed judgment that she sounded through the living room with a clear and heretofore untried resonance—"DO THE MATH. YOU'RE FIFTY. LET IT GO."—resonance fueled by two irritants: one, this call for increased stamina should interrupt Rachel Maddow's researched unraveling of the Trumpian horror of the day; and two, the woman in the commercial who would supposedly "like it too" was in her twenties while the man speaking into a mic to reporters (of this newsworthy event???) was in his forties. "SHE DOESN'T CARE ABOUT YOUR FUCKING PENIS. SHE THINKS YOU ARE AN OLD MAN." Marlee felt the rapscallion blood of satisfaction flow through her body after saying these words aloud as her husband sat on the other end of the couch, scrolling and saying nothing.

Yes, it was as if a great veil had been lifted to reveal the behind-the-scenes mechanism running this great show of the world or as if she had crept into the underbelly of it all to see the ragged slaves pushing the enormous cogs around and around, and she shook to the core when she realized she had been one of these cog-pushers all these years.

Lying in bed after sex one evening, Marlee asked (by all appearances out of curiosity and not for her survey of one), "Why do older men take Viagra?"

"Self-confidence. If I can get it up, I feel like a million smackers."

"It's okay if you can't get it up. It's a natural thing to stop getting it up."

"That seems so sad."

"That's where hugging comes in. Sex doesn't have to last forever."

"Yes, it does. Forever!" Her husband shot his fist in the air. Sex was an accomplishment. To achieve the accomplishment, he needed the mechanism: Marlee.

She turned over, grabbed her robe, and hauled herself to the bathroom to let semen drip out of her body for the millionth time and to pee to avoid a UTI while he grabbed his phone to scroll.

* * *

The general understanding in Marlee's society (USA, 2022) was that committed partners were to be sexually available for one another. That relationships required mutual sexual satisfaction. That Partner A touches or pulls or licks Partner B's part to make them feel something pleasant, even if Partner A feels as sexually dead as defrosted chicken while engaging in the act (but Partner A cannot express this fact to Partner B because it would destroy him. Instead, Partner A has to continue to do things and be things for Partner B. Partner A is feeling a swirling tempest form as month after year passes while she must continue to build up her fucking husba—Partner B.)

It's not that Marlee hadn't been aware of inequality and sexism and the patriarchy; she had experienced all of this from girlhood to this day. It was just that her new clarity uncovered the *degree* to which the world was saturated.

Getting ready for work, Marlee added color to her lips, and for the first time ever, her lips looked less than full, looked a bit thin. She lightened them with pink gloss and hated the anxiety she felt at the knowledge that her lips were closing in on themselves—a natural thing, but this natural thing meant dying, and to the office, it meant not as pretty. She hated that people looked at one another and labeled: pretty, ugly, young, old. Ultimately, she wished her lips fuller not because she wanted a man's approval but because she wanted her job and was afraid someone would take that away if every aspect of her physical being wasn't just so. But, as she dusted brown eyeshadow on her white roots, she thought the truth: If she lived alone with the bears in a cabin and had no monetary concerns, her lips would simply need to be moist so they wouldn't crack, and a smudge of coconut oil would do. And her hair, she'd never color because it was a royal pain in the ass. Though she'd probably still draw on her lost eyebrows until she was a bona fide old woman (shuffling, bent).

But she had a job. A damn good job with lots of money, relatively speaking, compared to years ago, and no credit card debt and a decent 401(k). The house was almost paid off. If needed, she could live by herself in her own apartment and be completely fine. Comfortable. If she wanted, she could move across the water, solo. She finally understood the archetypal woman with cat—both self-sufficient, each doing their own thing, neither asking the other for much. Here is kibble. Here is ear. A good book. A sweater. Bliss. No one needed to be jerked off to confirm they were still a man.

She capped her moisturizing lipstick and headed out the door. She'd park at the park-n-ride and catch a short bus to the ferry to Seattle.

Though the Bainbridge Ferry trip was always a tranquil journey, Marlee's new hormonal equilibrium created such peace within her during this day's trip that she had the idea, while lifting her gaze from her laptop to the placid Puget Sound, that she had reached the perfect human state. No pubescent flourishing, no adolescent appetite, no maternal worry, and no elderly frailty—which she imagined to be a trapping, holding a lifetime of wisdom inside a diminishing shell. Here, now, in her seat on the ferry, Marlee could think and do for herself without a single human or hormone pulling at her mind or body or heart.

The ferry docked, and the passengers headed off, Marlee leading the pedestrians. She had been standing at the door along with other fast walkers as the boat approached the pier. Some were runners, wearing gear, and some had buses to catch, like Marlee, but Marlee's preparedness was more than just her desire to be punctual; it was also due to the intoxication she always felt when hurtling through the city streets—especially now, having worked remotely for two years during the pandemic. Two months ago, she had picked up where she had left off, speeding like she used to, climbing Seattle blocks to her next ten-minute bus ride. Others would take the bus at the stop closer to the ferry, but she chose the walk, which she considered an essential part of her day, rain or shine, to keep fit and to be whipped to attention by the haphazard breezes from Elliott Bay, an umbrella always at the ready in her backpack.

Her route had changed since before the pandemic, both the streets she took and the streets themselves. Tall boards either hid or replaced tourist shops down Alaskan Way, creating a barrier between pedestrians and construction behind the boards on the water's edge. The change had started before the lockdown, when the Alaskan Way Viaduct, deemed unsafe, had been demolished. But in the sickly lull of this new world disease, while people and businesses died and waited and hoped, a tattered presence clung to these Seattle streets. An ominous and invisible presence, Marlee also felt. Maybe large rats crawled up through manholes at night. Maybe ribby dogs slunk low to the pavement. In the early morning daylight, a chalky feel lingered in the air, perhaps dust still holding on from the old viaduct, perhaps dirt wafting from the dragging of the many steps of the many homeless people who on some streets outnumbered the working ones because the working ones were working at home. Marlee thought as she avoided Marion Street because of a large tent-home of a street person and seeing many such people meandering and scratching all around, that most likely, there were not more homeless people as some were saying; we just saw more of them since the working bodies didn't block our view.

Marlee stayed on Alaskan Way then walked up Madison, always jaunty at 8:00 a.m., now more than ever with her newly acquired equilibrium, and when she made it to First Avenue, she paused at the light, which she always tried to beat but never could. Across the street, in front of the Henry M. Jackson Federal

Building, stood numerous people, mostly women, holding signs, and she knew at that moment this was the day: the Supreme Court leak had flooded her land. A few people in a room had decided, after discussions, that yes, the government could decide what to do with Marlee's body. As a matter of fact, fifty little governments could decide what to do with Marlee's body, depending on where she paid her mortgage.

The light at the street changed, but she remained. A woman with white hair and sloping shoulders held a sign at her belly. A man with no hair and floppy jowls held his hand-painted sign above his head. This crowd would grow.

The light changed again, and Marlee continued her walk up to Third Avenue much slower than before. She was one of the lucky ones: to live in a progressive state and to be too old to conceive.

Lucky or not, she still felt the weight of it all, knew the ramifications for the entire nation. She knew, too, that she would not be truly at peace until her own body was completely hers. *Sorry, hon. Don't take it personally, but I just don't want to have sex anymore.* Can you imagine? She thought the question in a mental conversation with herself. She shook her head as she trudged uphill, knowing that by simply uttering those words, a wedge would be drilled into her marriage. She had to choose to either be true to her body or to keep her husband content.

A construction truck rolled up the street. Fifty-two, and leers still landed on her body through vehicle windows, appraising what they felt was theirs to rate. How much inspection had she endured in her lifetime?

How many men's bodies had come her way? The ones she had invited and then regretted the arrival? The ones that persisted until she gave in? The necks that had hovered rhythmically over her face while she cried? The ones she was too young and drunk and lonely to walk away from? The diseases she should have? And the little pink daily pills she had thankfully popped from Planned Parenthood when she was eighteen, not because she was guided by a mentor or mother or nonexistent social media but quite by chance because a fellow student at school mentioned she was going. She had said it matter-of-factly with no shame or secrecy, and Marlee took on her aspect at that moment, wore it the day she entered the building. It had been a new thing to try on: *I would like to go on the pill.* And the response was easy and without judgment, just medical questions, income questions, an easy sliding scale, an exam, professionalism, information. The pill had protected her from her own unmoored, naïve, and lonely adolescence. Marlee didn't think much of herself all those years ago. The satisfaction and affection of the male of the month, her benchmark. It was the eighties. No one told young, skinny Marlee otherwise. No one told Marlee it was okay if a man didn't like her. Everyone told her men had to like her, and if they didn't, then she was worth little.

If fifty-two-year-old Marlee and eighteen-year-old Marlee should meet at an intersection like the one she was approaching, at Third and Madison, younger Marlee would smile, then look down, and she'd make room for older Marlee to walk. Older Marlee would smile in return and see the deference and feel tenderness for this young person, and she would break a little with worry that this girl-woman would be walked over, mostly by men, and ignored by women who would not know what to do with her because she was a little too pretty to have around and a little too nice and a little too lost. *Hey*, older Marlee hoped she would say, *You don't have to put up with that. Do you have some time? How much time do you have?* Older Marlee hoped she would stop everything she was about to do in her day and say, *Do you have all the time in the world for the most important information?*

Marlee crossed the street and walked to the end of the block, to Third and Seneca. She waved her ORCA card over the reader, and it accepted her fare with a beep. She was expected at a two-hour breakfast meeting with the board members. She readjusted her mask as the 70 bus made its way up the street. It squealed in front, and the doors opened. She saw her reflection in the glass, a working woman wearing a light-blue mask under tired eyes, a woman who had little say in the scheme of things, yet her life had meant something to at least a handful of humans, and lately, more than ever, it meant something to her.

*Let's go, Marlee.* She turned around and walked the way she had come. *There is so much you need to know before you make all those bad decisions. Let me give you some guidance, a plan book you may or may not follow completely, but at least it will give you possibilities.*

Marlee made it to First Avenue and joined the crowd. She had no sign. She had such thoughts, though. Finally, the time had come. Women did not need men. A woman's livelihood was more important than a man's kindness or smiles, which were fleeting. Her dependence would be her downfall. She needed to make her own money, and doing so would give her power over herself. This was the key, she was sure.

And as she read the sign "Our Bodies, Our Lives," she thought of the many times she wanted to leave her marriage.

How she wasn't happy but had settled because she had these babies who became kids who loved their dad, and they loved her, too. She didn't want to hurt them—their sweet brows and their tenderness—and she knew if she were to leave, then her children would never be the same, and she just couldn't do that. So she stayed, committed to making sure they had a good life. She's been at this for twenty-five years, and she then realized, quite suddenly and with horror, that having a baby was potentially, quite possibly, probably, and yes, most definitely, a long, long road to complete dependence. And she cleared her throat and opened her mouth.

* * *

# Discussion Questions

1. Do you think a married spouse has an obligation to have sex even when they aren't in the mood? What if they are *never* in the mood?
2. What do you think is the cause of Marlee's lack of interest in having sex with her husband? Is there something she can change about her life to regain her sex drive?
3. Barring a medical condition, if a person doesn't ever want to have sex with their partner, does that mean their relationship is failing, or can couples have a fulfilling, sexless relationship?
4. Do women who make more money, have more self-confidence, and seek less approval from men naturally want less, more, or the same amount of sex?
5. Marlee says children are a road to dependence. What does this mean, and do you agree?

* * *

# Yellow Is the Color of Choices

## *Penny Milam*

\* \* \*

For whatever reason, when she sees me each weekend, Megan still hugs me like when she was five. Her skinny arms wrap around my waist, and her eyes squeeze tight like she's absorbing me into her skin. This is both heartening and heart-wrenching. I want her to miss me. I hate being a thing she has to miss. "Hey, baby girl," I gush in a high, enthusiastic voice. "Long time, no see." Her head rests in the center of my chest, where it reached two summers ago and grew no taller. I kiss the messy brown hair. It smells faintly unwashed.

Megan appears on my doorstep like a hallucination every Friday night, the retreating purr of her mom's car soundtracking her entrance to my empty apartment. I am somewhat amazed that at fourteen, she still chooses to spend her weekends with me. I hoard these golden moments, polishing the memory of them on a hectic Tuesday morning or during a lonely Wednesday lunch hour. They remind me there is more to my life than an indifferent job and a string of complaining voicemails from Megan's mom—my ex—The Bitch.

"What're we gonna do this weekend?" Megan asks as she dumps her backpack at the door of her bedroom. She has clothes in the closet and stuffed animals on the dresser, but I never see them move. She totes her "real" clothes from home, and she always brings along Bunny, a much-loved gray washrag of a rabbit she's had since she was two. My room for her is as sterile as a motel—convenient when it gets too late to go home, but nowhere she actually wants to hang out. I try to come up with places to entertain her during our time together. I hope she'll remember those instead of the musty bedsheets that don't smell like her. Mostly, I'm just frantic to fill the hours of two people who are determined to love each other despite no longer knowing each other very well. "I thought we could go to the movies tomorrow." I settle onto the sofa, and she snuggles beside me like she's done since she was a toddler. God, I love her.

"Sure," she says against my shirt. "Maybe we could do the farmer's market too? I can get some stuff to make us smoothies."

I hate the farmer's market—overly-friendly vendors, squelching, muddy walkways, the haunting undertone of rotting vegetables flooding my nose with the tidal allergy-scratch of illicit death. We go because Megan adores it, and the too-few weekends I spend with her flood me with their own tides of guilt. "Whatever you want, baby girl."

Her mom's on some "all-natural" kick and, apparently, their house—my old house—is now filled to the brim with smoothies and kale salads and super-foods. My apartment kitchen is full of Little Debbies and coffee, which I'm told with a pitying smile from my daughter will kill me or, worse, make me fat. In her concern, I hear the superior tone of her mother. my ex—The Bitch.

In the blinding summer light of morning, we arrive at the farmer's market set up in rows on the courthouse lawn, her steps bouncing and mine resigned. It rained yesterday, and within minutes, my sneakers are caked in mud. Megan has the sense to wear galoshes, a thin, tan link of skin stretching between her pink shorts and the high rubber top of the shoes. The boots have chickens on them.

My daughter ping-pongs between stalls, and I watch her like a favorite movie. Seeing her only a few days a week, she seems to age in fast-forward. Already, she's outgrowing the shirt she bought the first of May, even though it's barely July. She needs a haircut, too, but maybe she told me she was trying to grow it long? She looks like a child to me, though by the glances she's getting from men my own age, I recognize she is not. Perverts. How can they not see the sweet innocence in her? It's the only innocence left in my life.

She leads me to a stall that sells raw honey, and behind the counter is a kid whose face glows neon pink at the sight of her. I realize our trip has an ulterior motive; I've been manipulated. Megan pulls me forward to meet him; I hate him at once.

"Tyson, this is my dad. Dad, Tyson goes to my school. He's a senior." She says the last as if it's an accomplishment no one has ever achieved before. My image of him skews. His grin is no longer goofy but predatory; Tyson is no longer a kid but a grown man looking at my baby in a way I recognize from the men we passed along the way. He smiles with no trace of fear, holding out his hand to shake mine as men do.

"Nice to meet you, Dr. Emerson."

Megan says, "I told him you were a pharmacist," and Tyson nods. "I think that's really cool. I've thought about going into medicine myself."

"Really?" He doesn't acknowledge my skepticism.

"I guess I've got a few years to decide about med school, though."

"Not as many as Megan," I point out, and he considers it seriously. "That's true."

"Tyson is a beekeeper," Megan hands me one of the mason jars pyramided on the table. I examine the honeycomb through the warped glass. Deep within the amber lava flow, the corpse of a bee hangs suspended. "He raises them and collects the honey all by himself."

"That right."

Tyson nods and ducks his head as if embarrassed at Megan's praise. "I've been doing it for a few years now."

"Uh-huh." I don't know what else to say, though they are clearly waiting for me to add to the conversation. "Well, I'd love to try some." My high, enthusiastic voice is back. "How much?"

Tyson shakes his head; I've offended him. "No, sir, I wouldn't dream of charging you! Take it! I know how much Meg loves honey."

"We couldn't take it without paying for it." I toss a twenty on the table where it remains between us, a dog turd no one wants to clean up. "Sounds like you've worked pretty hard, and you're probably saving up... for med school." The rubber-band smile on my face stretches thin, close to snapping. Tyson ducks his head again. "Well, I appreciate it." He doesn't touch the bill; he'll pocket it after I'm gone. I enjoy that he'll take no pleasure in it.

"Would you mind if I stayed here with Tyson for a little bit?" Megan clasps her hands in prayer and offers me pleading eyes. "He says this time of day gets real busy, and he could use the help." I'm not only manipulated; I'm betrayed. I glance around at the slow pace of the Saturday shoppers—there is no rush in our small town for anything, much less jars of honey. I check my watch. "Well, we have to go soon if we want to make that movie. Maybe a half an hour?"

She is delighted and practically hops the table to stand beside him. Instead of three of us, it has transformed into a clearly-defined couple and me. "It was nice to meet you, Dr. Emerson."

"You, too, Tyler."

"It's *Tyson*, Dad." Megan is quick to correct me. I swear it wasn't on purpose.

"Of course." I step away with the mason jar of honey weighing heavy in my grip. I have been dismissed.

* * *

The first weekend Megan misses, she claims she's at a friend's for a sleepover. The second weekend, she has a big test to study for. The third weekend, she admits through a text that she has a date with Tyson. If The Bitch and I were still married, I'd get to see my daughter every night, and these lost weekends wouldn't hurt so badly. Because it's natural, right? She's supposed to like boys and crush on them and want to spend all her time with them.

I suspect The Bitch encourages Megan to miss her allotted

time with me. It would be just like her to whittle away the hours until we don't see each other at all. According to Megan, her mom thinks Tyson is wonderful, and *she* sees no problem with the four-year age gap, which, at this age, may as well be twenty. The man who shook my hand isn't the same brand of innocence as my baby girl is—he knows things. Not even things he shouldn't know, just things I don't think my daughter should. But finally, on the fourth weekend, she shows up again like springtime.

She never just comes through the front door like she has a right to; she always knocks. I open the door, and she almost leaps into my arms. She hugs me tight, and everything feels right again. And then I see her eyes.

They are still bright, still happy, but there is a difference in them. A knowledge that cannot be hidden. I hate Tyson with cold fury as my baby girl drops her backpack at her door and plops down on the couch beside me. She's too young for this, I think, ignoring my own past and her mother's even. I ignore the memory of feeling like we'd been granted the secrets of the universe. And look where it got us. A divorce, a bitter hatred, tainted memories, and one fourteen-year-old between us. A fourteen-year-old who won't want to hear her feelings might not last, or love may not burn forever.

She doesn't want to go anywhere tonight, she tells me. "Let's just watch a movie and order pizza, okay?" Fine with me. We turn on *The Wizard of Oz*, one of her childhood favorites, and eat pepperoni pizza out of the box; for a moment, my world balances on normality.

It's not until we are cleaning up and she's already brushed her teeth and changed into pajamas that she works up her nerve.

"Dad, I have to tell you something."

I freeze, my arms half-crushing the pizza box into the garbage can. She stands in the doorway in striped pjs, and I kid you not, Bunny held in the crease of her arm as she drops the bomb. "I'm going to have a baby."

The pizza box flies across the room to leave a greasy skid mark on the wall. An inhuman sound foghorns from my mouth. "That son of a bitch! I'll kill him!" Echoes of horrible things bounce around the room until they become static and color. I tell her I'm disappointed in her. I tell her she's a moron for not using protection. I call him a child molester. I don't remember all the other things I spew; I choose not to remember. I make her cry.

The tears pierce my anger, and I deflate. I try to pull her close and apologize, but she has grown hard and prickled like she possesses a dozen elbows and knees. She hugs the doorframe as I backpedal. "Baby, I'm sorry. You just shocked me."

"Mom said you'd react like this."

"Your mom knows?"

"Of course. She's the one who told me to tell you tonight." She wipes snot on her pajama sleeve and won't look me in the eye. "She said you'd be furious, but I didn't believe her."

I get a grip on my rage. "How did your mom react?"

Megan clutches Bunny tighter. "She said it wasn't ideal, but she didn't really have room to talk since you and she did the same thing." Her face becomes crafty, and I catch the wily glimpse of her mother.

"We did, and it changed our whole lives." I sit down at the table and put my head in my hands.

She inches closer to me and takes a seat at the table too. "That's what she said. She didn't lose her cool, though." The accusation stings.

"Does Tyson know? I assume it's Tyson's." I insult her with the question, and she stiffens.

"Of course it is! And not yet. I'm seeing him Monday, and I'll tell him then."

I sift through options, looking for a solution, wishing for an eraser. "You don't have to. We can make an appointment this week, and he never has to know." My voice sharpens. "Or maybe he *should* know, help pay for it. He shouldn't get out of this scot-free, after all."

"What are you talking about?" She breaks my focus. "An appointment for what?"

"Baby, I only meant—"

"You think I would kill this baby? Mine and Tyson's?" Static and color flood the room again, her rage this time, not mine.

"It isn't a baby," I contradict; my throat chokes on the word. The word is a spell. If I name it, then it *becomes*. "Not really, not yet. It's a bad decision and a bunch of cells that can ruin your life."

"Is that what you wish you'd done back then? Made a good decision? Get rid of a 'bunch of cells'?" She takes on a nastiness I've only heard in The Bitch's voice before. "Those bunch of cells were me! Do you wish you'd killed me?"

"Megan, please, that's not what I'm saying..."

"I won't kill my baby! Tyson wouldn't want it either! I can't believe you! How could you think that?" And she runs from the room.

It takes me several minutes to think again. For a while, I just float in that static and color, seeing my future, her future, slip away from me. I doubt Tyson is going to want this baby, either. He has plans, and they don't include a fourteen-year-old and a newborn. I allow myself to burn against The Bitch's sabotage to make me out as a villain for trying to solve this without destroying Megan's life. But after only a few short breaths, I realize Megan is right. We hadn't aborted the pregnancy; instead, we got married at twenty, struggled for years to survive on love and minimum wage. I worked at a grocery store to pay the bills through undergrad and then shifts at night so I could go to pharmacy school during the day. The Bitch and I grew to hate each other as the days filled with separate hours and separate interests. Finally, my job paid well, but the damage was long done. Years of living off of credit ruined our bank accounts, and my being away from home gutted our relationship, if we'd ever had one. Megan sees herself in that plus sign on the stick, her entire existence mirrored in my past and in her present. But I see reflections upon reflections of that single choice.

I wait until I don't hear crying in her bedroom before I try again to talk with her. I sit down on the bed where she lies like a clenched fist of despair with Bunny in her lap, and I gently lay out the future for her with a baby. I explain the long nights, the financial hardship, the strain on her health and her future plans. I am calm and soft-spoken, and she listens. When I finish, she meets my eyes, and I see a glimpse of the adult she will one day become—too soon, much too soon. "No, Dad. There is no decision to make because it's already been made. I'm keeping my baby. I don't know what Tyson will expect, but I'll tell him the same thing. I'll do this on my own if I have to." She, too, knows the power of naming a thing, the spell that she is attempting to conjure.

As if the choice is hers alone. She can't even legally have a job yet, but she's going to take care of a child? What she really means is that her mom and I are going to have to. She has a make-believe view of life, and I'm either cast as a fairy godfather or as the ogre. For the moment, I nod along. "All right, Megan. I hear you. Let's get some sleep for now, and we'll talk about it in the morning."

"There's nothing to talk about," she warns me. "I won't change my mind, and you can't make me kill my baby." The tears reappear in her eyes, and I lean over to kiss the top of her head. I leave the room and turn off the light. A butterfly nightlight shines dimly at ankle level.

* * *

I call The Bitch but should have known better. While I have to keep my voice down, she has no such restrictions. She is bitter, vindictive, vocal.

*It's your fault for not watching her closely enough.*

*I'm not the one who left us.*

*It's your fault for not being here.*

*Are you happy now?*

*It's your fault.*

*Hypocrite.*

The Bitch has no qualms about abortions, but I know she wants Megan to keep it with the same selfish, short-sightedness as my daughter. It will cause me pain, which she enjoys. There is no convincing her to side together to convince Megan to make the right choice—once again, it is a clearly defined couple against me alone. I hang up with an unsatisfying punch of a button.

The next day is Saturday, and I go into the office in the fresh, pink-filtered sunlight of dawn. The decision was made in the stark hours of the night, and I do not hesitate now. I write a prescription and fill it myself—mifepristone and misoprostol. Those years of nighttime grocery-store bagging were not wasted. When I get home, I wake a bleary-eyed Megan and hand her the first pill with a glass of water.

"What's this?" she asks in groggy confusion. I lie easily.

"It's an iron pill. If you plan on having this baby, you'll need to start taking these every few days to build up your strength."

Her face transforms, and she hugs me in a five-year-old's hug once again. I am reborn as her savior. She happily takes the pill, and I tell her we should take it easy this weekend. She agrees but springs out of bed with amazing energy, her life suddenly expanding before her in sunlight and kittens and fairy-tale endings.

We watch another family favorite—*The Sound of Music*—while she munches on popcorn, and I keep an eye on the time. When six hours pass, I pull out a blister packet of pills.

"What's that?" she asks with no suspicion in her voice.

"It's a prenatal vitamin," I say. "There's lots of them on the market, but they're all different. This is a new one that you put in your cheek and suck on for half an hour. You only have to take it once a week, though, so it's easier. If you are serious about this, you'll have to start a routine to... take care of the baby." The future planning makes it believable.

New responsibilities emanate from her face in ferocious

joy. "I will!" She never questions me, never considers that her father might be lying. That very fact solidifies my purpose. I rattle the yellow pills in the palm of my hand; she tucks them between her cheeks and gums.

I sit in the dark for hours until finally, she appears at my bed, crying and clutching her stomach. "Something's wrong," she whispers. In the bathroom, she curls up on the floor, this time a clenched fist of fear, as her uterus expels the inconvenient obstacle to her future. I hold her forehead as she cries, and Bunny watches from the bedroom across the hall. At the end of the night, nothing is left inside her but promise. Sometime in the future, she will learn the truth and may hate me for it. Or she may be secretly glad. For the present moment, she is safe. "Daddy!" She mourns her baby.

I comfort mine. "I'm so sorry, baby girl," I whisper against her hair. "Sometimes in life, we can't choose what happens."

* * *

# Discussion Questions

1. Does Megan, as a fourteen-year-old, have the right to decide what happens to her unborn baby? Is there some age or situation in which the prospective mother shouldn't be the primary decider? Does it matter she isn't even old enough to legally have a job?

2. Do you think Megan's father did the right thing by tricking her into aborting the baby? What (if anything) do you think he should have done instead?

3. To what extent is Megan's father acting in Megan's best interest, and to what extent is he trying to prevent the mistake he made at her age with "The Bitch" that leads to an unhappy marriage and divorce? Does his having mixed motivations matter?

4. Are Megan's parents responsible for her pregnancy because of their lack of educating Megan or because of their failure to role model a healthy marriage? Does their respective fault create an obligation in them to help Megan support her new child?

5. If you were Megan in this story and years later found out what your father did, would you be angry at him? Could you forgive him? Would you thank him?

* * *

# W h o s e   L i f e   I s   I t

## *Deborah Serra*

\* \* \*

"What the hell?" Danny jumped up and tore out of the kitchen where he'd been reading his mail and enjoying a quiet lunch with his sister, Elaine. Startled, she looked up from the newspaper.

"Danny?"

He ran through the foyer, out the front door, and then leaped down the three porch steps. He was in good shape for his age. And even though Elaine had no shoes on, she chased after him, alarmed.

"Danny, stop! What's happening?"

Something was seriously wrong. So wrong that her brother could do nothing but run—not talk, not explain, not even make eye contact, simply run toward the driveway. So, she ran after him—shoeless. Elaine felt every single sticky desiccated foxtail and spikey burr she stepped on, but she didn't slow down because Danny's desperation was fuel. He wrenched open the driver's side door of his Ford F150 with such force she thought he might pull it from the hinges.

"Danny!"

"Get in the car!"

The car was in gear when Elaine slid into the passenger seat. She caught her breath as she slammed shut the door of the now moving truck. Danny was known as the worst driver in the family. This was settled family lore. He crashed one family car after a long shift at work when he dozed off at the wheel, and he drove into the rear bumper of another at a red light when he reached for his phone. He was backing up now at such a speed that Elaine feared distracting him, so she kept quiet for the moment. She bit the inside of her mouth and held onto the door handle.

Plenty of times over the years, Danny had reacted dramatically. Just last year, she'd been with him at the DMV; he had turned seventy years old and was required to renew his license in person, which he found insulting and a waste of his time. He told both of his sisters, the information lady at the desk, and the twenty people in line ahead of him, that the older you got. the less time you had, and other people should not be allowed to waste it, which made a little bit of sense, actually. Stalled in the DMV line, he became so irritated he started singing the National Anthem very loudly to see if anyone would react. Most people took a few furtive steps away giving him more space, which Elaine found totally understandable, but two Marines sitting in plastic chairs waiting for their IDs abruptly stood up. They looked perplexed doing it, and it made Danny grin. But this? This? This balls-out running and reckless backing down the driveway was dangerous. This was a whole new level of dramatic, and Elaine felt frightened. She regretted her decision to jump into his truck. Looking back over his shoulder, Danny screeched to the end of the driveway, yanked the steering wheel, and spun it in such a way that Elaine's head hit the side window.

"Ow, Danny, stop. What are you doing?"

"Hold on." And he hit the accelerator with way too much force. Elaine's head snapped back, and she knew a neck strain and headache were in her future.

Elaine would've yelled, but she was fraught. She wasn't sure talking to him was the right thing. He was going 50 mph in a 20-mph zone, so she knew something needed to be said, but anything could be a distraction. She felt dampness spreading under her armpits and at her hairline. She reached down and pulled a sharp foxtail from the side of her foot, which began to bleed. She tried to calm down and consider her options. Then, she spoke carefully.

"Daniel, you need to tell me what's going on."

"I need to focus." And he took the corner on two wheels.

"Then, let me out. Give me your phone and let me out."

"Can't stop."

Danny reached into his pants pocket and...

"Both hands on the wheel! Danny, both hands."

He pulled a creased and crumbled letter from his pocket. It was the one he'd been reading at the table. He tossed it to Elaine. She looked. The envelope was addressed to them both.

"What's this?" Elaine didn't know whether to open and read the note in her hand or to keep her attention on the road. Under the circumstances, an extra pair of eyes was a plus.

"Read it, Elaine."

"Only if you slow down!"

"I'm not slowing down. Wait. First, call Claire."

"Why?"

"CALL!"

Elaine hit their sister's phone number.

"Hi, this is Claire; I'm not returning messages. Have a beautiful day."

"Voicemail."

"Call 911."

"Daniel, either you tell me what's going on right now, or I'll call 911 and report you."

"Read the letter."

Elaine opened the note and read.

*Dear Friends & Family, I want you to know how very much I appreciate your love and kindness. I've had such a wonderful life. A Wonderful Life: Frank Capra and James Stewart, right? Anyway, as you know, I've always been a Frank Sinatra fan, and now, at seventy-two years old, what I want is to do this My Way. (So many entertainment references I hadn't expected.) Please know that I'm fine. I really am absolutely fine. I know exactly what I'm doing. I'm sane. I'm healthy. But I'm bored. Bored to the bone. Bored with it all. Bored with getting up, with making food, with watching TV, with restaurants and laundry, with airports and gardening, with shopping and every conversation sounding the same. I know I've joked over the years that I didn't ever want to get old and ugly—except, yes, here's the spoiler: I wasn't joking. Please respect this decision and try to understand this is what I want. There's no heartache. I'm just done here. It's good to know when you're done. No sadness. Simply done. Everything you need to know about my affairs is on a list on my desk. Don't leave me hanging around for too long! HA! Have a lovely life. Thank you both for everything. Please don't grieve. Party for me. Ciao, Claire.*

Elaine's eyes stayed on the page as the intent seeped in. Then, she folded the note with unusual care as though it was the most precious thing she owned. As Danny sped through the streets, she folded it in half, smoothed it out on her leg, folded it in quarters, smoothed it out again. And then she sat, staring, as her mind replayed snippets of things Claire had said over the years: *the day I can't wear heels anymore, I'm done; the day my neck looks rooster-like, I'm done; the day I wake up bored, I'm done; the day I feel no purpose, I'm done.* They had all laughed at her when she said these things.

Elaine carefully slid the letter into her jeans. Suddenly, she didn't notice how wild or fitfully Danny was driving. She felt a strange mental and emotional paralysis. It was as though something was being worked out behind her face in the back of her mind, and she needed to wait for it. She felt elevated and immobile. She was looking down on herself, and her brain felt paused. They were only a few blocks away now.

"Call her again. Then, 911."

Elaine didn't move.

"Elaine? Elaine, are you okay? Call Claire again and then 911."

"I don't think so."

"What?"

"No. She's gone."

"Don't give up. There may be time to help her. To stop her."

Elaine looked out the window at the passing trees, "Should we?"

Danny yanked the car into the cul-de-sac where Claire lived in an apartment at the end of the block.

"I know you're upset. We need to focus, Elaine."

"This note is pretty clear, Danny. She's done."

"Don't you get it? This is a suicide note!"

"I can see that, but it seems thoughtful, like this is what she wants, what she chooses."

"I'm her brother. I can talk to her. She's having a tough moment, is all. I can fix this."

"Doesn't sound like a tough moment. Sounds pretty thought through."

Danny slammed on the brakes as he pulled into the apartment complex drive. He jumped out of the truck and raced up the outside stairs to Claire's apartment. Elaine followed more slowly now.

At the apartment door, Danny pounded. "Claire! Claire! It's Danny. Open up."

"Look at the postmark. She sent this four days ago."

"Oh, god." Danny dialed 911.

"What is your emergency? Fire, paramedics, or police?"

"Both. All of them. My sister is killing herself, and I'm going to break down the door now."

"Please wait for law enforcement."

"No time. Send help."

Danny kicked hard at the front door. It didn't budge. He took a few steps back to try again. He kicked it as hard as he could and then screamed out in pain. He'd broken his foot. He slumped to the floor in front of the door and knocked again loudly with a cry in his voice.

"Claire, please, please open the door."

Elaine slid down next to her brother. Tears in both their eyes.

"The police will be here in a few minutes. The station's right down the road." Elaine tried to comfort him.

"We're too late, aren't we."

"I think so."

"This is wrong. This is a crime, or a sin, or stupid, or all three. How could she do this?"

"Remember in high school when we read *The Myth of Sisyphus*? I think it was Camus. Well, whoever it was, they wrote about how if you have no purpose, if you feel life is meaningless, then suicide is the obvious choice."

"Bullshit. There's purpose. There's her brother and sister, our feelings, her friends, a good cup of coffee in the morning, or a walk on the beach. There's lots of purpose. There's purpose all over the damn place!"

"She has no one depending on her, Danny, no children, her husband long gone. Do we have the right to require her to stay here for us?"

"Life is the reason. Life is the purpose. She's hurting people. She's hurting us."

"I'll miss her too."

"It's selfish and mean."

"Is she the one being selfish?"

"Yes."

"We don't choose to be born or to get old, to have a healthy body or a sound mind. Seems this is the only truly personal and significant choice a person can make about their fundamental life. I don't like it, but I think she had that right. To make that private decision. The right to say goodbye when she wanted and on her own terms."

"She did not have that right! Life is a gift."

"A gift she returned."

"How could you be snide at a moment like this? Our sister is dead inside this apartment."

"I know. I know." Now, they were both crying. "But this was well-planned. This was not one bad moment."

The siren could be heard approaching.

Danny looked down at his broken foot. "It's swelling. Help me get this shoe off."

Elaine gently removed Danny's shoe. His foot was already turning color.

Danny and Elaine sat there with their backs up against Claire's front door, crying and close enough to feel each other's breath on their faces. Elaine whispered, "I don't think people should have to go on living for other people. She was done. I'm sad for me, but this was her life. I will respect her choice."

"I will never forgive her."

* * *

# Discussion Questions

1.  At the end of the story, Elaine says, "I don't think people should have to go on living for other people." Do you agree or disagree? Do we have an obligation to continue living for the sake of those who love us? Who need us?

2.  Do you think Claire was wrong in leaving a letter rather than talking to her family before killing herself? Should she have given them the time to properly say goodbye?

3.  Is a life without purpose meaningless? What qualifies as a life with purpose? Does the simple pleasure of drinking a morning cup of coffee count, or must it be more?

4.  What restrictions (if any) should be placed on someone for them to be allowed to commit suicide? Must they have a painful, terminal disease, or can they just be over it all and ready to die? Should there be a minimum age requirement?

5.  If you arrived at Claire's house and found her unconscious from her suicide attempt but still alive, would you call 911 in an attempt to save her or wait a bit to give her time to pass?

* * *

# R e a c h

## *Mark Braidwood*

* * *

Jack Benson stands dissolved in an ocean of strangers, humans he couldn't have known existed until forced to jostle with them for space and shared odors. He recoils imperceptibly with each touch, eager not to offend or stand out any further. As a mass, they flow like a tide, but he senses that, as individuals, each is preoccupied with being elsewhere.

He marvels at this accretion of humanity, at how in each moment, somewhere on Earth, such a mass of people goes about their day. Who are they? What do they want, feel, do with their lives? The man next to him smells of cigarettes and holds a child's doll. He looks nervous. Perhaps it's been a while since he saw her. He wonders if there is a set of personality archetypes such that it's possible to know every type of person that has ever existed, if only you could map them onto the right template.

This thought had struck him while on the plane. He had sat next to someone—round-backed, in his forties and dressed in brown chinos and a blue turtleneck, no doubt middle management in some tech company—whom he felt he had met so many times before, the way he introduced himself unprompted, assured of the pleasure of his own company.

Finally, the customs desk looms above him, the throng's singular objective. He hands over his passport.

"Mr. Benson, what is the point of your visit?" the immigration officer asks.

"Business."

The officer stares at him and again at his passport. Was his suspicion an act or learned from experience? "How long?"

His cheeks redden and his heart quickens. What he's doing isn't illegal. Not where he is from. "A few days."

The officer returns his passport and waves him through, his mask degrading briefly into indifference, boredom, or perhaps fatigue.

His employer had arranged for someone to meet him. It hadn't been difficult to justify this detour from his itinerary, the department head thinking it positive for their corporate image. They briefed him not to trust anyone, that there was every chance the people he met with would work for the party, whatever that meant.

A row of men in ill-fitting suits surround the exit, holding signs with names hastily scrawled across paper, some in English, others Chinese. He finds his name printed on a white placard, held by a muscular man with dark hair and tanned skin, standing a little apart from the others.

"Mr. Benson, welcome to Guangdong. My name is Wei. May I take your bag?"

His English is excellent, not the kind picked up begrudgingly in school or from watching reruns of American soaps, but the kind cultivated with prolonged effort. Did that mean he was good at his job or had another job entirely?

Jack thanks him. The man seems surprised at how light his bag is, perhaps used to fifty-pound monsters. But the only important thing, the reason he is here, is folded in his top pocket.

The car is parked at the pickup area. He sits in the back.

"Which hotel, sir?"

"I'd like to go straight to this address, please." He holds out his phone and the driver squints as he reads. His eyebrows rise slightly, perhaps at the unexpected address or the distance.

"I can pay."

"Thank you, but that won't be necessary." The man had a large flask from which he sipped constantly, the smell hinting at some kind of tea.

It was supposed to be easy, finding this place. Just ask Charlie Pringle, someone had suggested. Unlike his own workspace, which had a weeping fig in the corner and a print of Klimt's Beech Forest on the wall, Charlie had arranged his favorite toys around his office. He had tried hard not to judge him.

"How can I help?" Charlie asked with bright eyes.

"Where do we manufacture the K-Bot? Need to chase something up."

Charlie frowned, swiveled in his chair and tapped away at his computer. After a while, he turned back.

"As I thought. Don't know."

"I don't understand," Jack said.

"Same with most of our lines. We outsource it to someone on the ground."

"I see. Can you ask them?"

Charlie shook his head. "They won't know either."

"Jesus, don't we know where we make our own toys?"

Charlie's eyes narrowed.

"I'm going to China to meet with our suppliers," Jack explained. "Thought I might tour some factories while there."

It took Charlie two weeks to locate it.

As they leave the airport, the city reads like a coming-of-age story in reverse. The downtown buildings rendered in sleek lines and gleaming surfaces, rows standing tall with the aggressive symmetry of collector's cabinets, contents stuffed, segregated and cataloged. Did it ever happen that somebody confused their home for another's, mistakenly entering a copy of their apartment? He smiles. Could someone accidentally adopt a new life, a new family? Glimpses of great gouges in the earth rush past the window, waiting to be healed by concrete and steel. Further along, older dwellings cling to the banks of a muddy river, a mosaic of color and shape, a jumble of crossed paths and perhaps shared fates. Occasionally he glimpses empty fields in the distance.

It was odd how long it had taken him to think of translating the note. He'd guessed it was Chinese and had taken it to Jo-An in HR, who grew up there. She looked at the photograph he had taken of the small piece of paper, torn from a notebook. The original was too precious and might raise questions.

She squinted, her lips moving silently before she spoke. "Okay. This is a short poem."

"What does it say?"

She read aloud.

*Thunder rolls*
*Leaves hang heavy,*
*I bow my head.*

\* \* \*

It wasn't what he had expected and now even more out of place.

"Is that it?"

"Yep. Told you it was short. It's nice. Who wrote it?"

"I... I don't know," he said. "My niece found it. For a school project. Just curious is all."

"It is curious."

"In what way?"

"Well, its form is reminiscent of Japanese haiku, but it's written in Mandarin."

He had imagined a plea for help or bearing witness to some crime. Instead, a poem.

He kept her hastily scrawled English translation and regularly returned to it, perhaps hoping the freshness of another read might reveal a clue. Each time he read it, he was reminded of when his parents took him for walks in the forest—the one that is now a shopping mall—and the smell of rain soaking into the ground, of a wet leaf brushing against his cheek. He had started reading haiku and Chinese poetry, but the secret note remained his favorite.

After almost an hour, they reach the area of the city where the factories sprawl, the cogs and gears of wealth buttressing the entire edifice, alchemists turning lead into gold. He begins to taste the soot that clings to everything.

"We're here," his driver says. "I'll take you in."

They park outside a dirty gray multi-story office building

dwarfed by the large attached annex. Inside the office he is met by a man and a woman: the site manager, in his forties with a middle bulge to match his status, and the daughter of the company's founder, a stout woman with graying hair. To Jack's relief, she speaks English. His driver does not introduce himself.

As they show him around, the woman talks about how the company started making Christmas tree decorations. They walk deeper into the factory. He begins to doubt himself. If word got back to the office about what he was trying to do here, what would they think? Worse, could he be mistaken for a human rights activist? Workers' conditions are a touchy subject. Was it too late to turn back? His family knows he's here but not why. Such a strange thing to find, he'd chosen to keep it to himself.

It had been the Christmas just gone. He had finished adding the brandy to the eggnog and had sat down to watch the kids prowl around the base of the tree. Even though it almost touched the ceiling, the stack of presents around its base somehow made the tree look small. An *embarras de richesses*, his wife might say if she were to notice.

He and his wife had bought this house just after they married. Since then, they'd had two kids and watched the neighborhood change as older residents died and their children moved away, as the houses gained a level or were replaced altogether.

"The kids want to start, honey," he called.

"Go ahead, I'll be a little while."

Which of these toys would become inseparable from his children such that he would need to know their whereabouts at all times, and which would end up in the basement after a few days, stored until they could be donated, given away or, as was typical, discarded?

Richmond, the eldest, had already opened one of his presents, holding up the colorful plastic robot like a trophy kill.

"What does it do?"

"It talks and follows commands. Your friends will think it's great."

Richmond quickly found the ON button and pressed it. Nothing happened.

"It doesn't work."

"Keep trying, sweetheart. It comes with batteries."

When it didn't do anything, his interest flagged, and he dropped the toy at his feet and moved on, tearing into the paper wrapping of the next present in his pile.

Jack got out of his chair and picked up the robot. It definitely wasn't working. Larry from marketing had said it would be a sure thing. He unscrewed the back. The batteries were not sitting properly; wedged underneath was a piece of paper. He unfolded it.

As they make their way through the factory, he controls his anxiety by asking questions, feigning interest in every detail. Finally, they reach the control room. He meets the foreman and draws out a conversation about forecasting, scheduling, and capacity planning as much as he is able. It seems he can't bore either of them.

"May I watch the factory for a while?"

She smiles, eager to please. He turns his back on her and pretends to be engrossed in the view from the window that overlooks the factory floor. Hundreds of workers sit in a large room lit by strips of fluorescent tubes suspended from the ceiling, their hands in constant motion as they assemble the final product from parts manufactured elsewhere.

He has gambled that this would be the best stage in manufacturing to hide a note. It would be too risky any earlier. Some of the toy parts on the assembly line are familiar, so he at least has the correct factory. But what are the chances the poem's author is here? His stomach tightens, and his mouth is suddenly dry. What a fool he has been to think he could find the person, and what did he hope to achieve if he did? Continuing to watch is all he can think to do.

After it is clear he intends to watch for a while, they excuse themselves, probably wondering about this strange foreigner, and leave him with his driver and the foreman. His driver's gaze roams around the room. Surely, he would need the bathroom eventually. He had drunk almost a liter of tea during the drive.

After ten minutes of silence, from the corner of his view, a flicker of irritation, of involuntary movement toward the door. Here it is. The driver takes one last look around the room, then excuses himself.

Jack crosses over to the foreman.

"Do you speak English?"

He shrugs.

Jack pulls out an envelope fat with Yuan, calculated to be the equivalent of a month's wage. The man's eyes open wide.

He hands him the poem, moves back to the windows, points and says, "Read." The foreman's face is hard to judge, but he walks over to a microphone, checking the door behind.

The words of the poem boom across the factory floor, the speakers easily overcoming the noise of machinery. The effect is immediate. A woman erupts from anonymity, standing bolt upright. About his age, thin and tired, eyes wide and flicking about.

Jack bangs on the glass. Their eyes meet. The tiny muscles in her face compose stanzas that flow from recognition to surprise, from wonder to fear. A message sent and received. Perhaps a friendship never realized.

He longs to reach out to her as she did to him, to tell her how he often reads her message. Jack smiles, but the moment is lost. She sits down and bows her head, reclaimed by her chore.

Who did she see? A stranger who crossed an ocean to find the hand that penned a note hidden inside a child's toy? Her strong hands resume their motion between the conveyor belt and her workstation. Where else have her poems traveled? He wonders suddenly if he might belong to a secret club, its members touched by this woman's yearning.

Other workers are looking at her. A man on the factory floor is pointing up at him. Jack has put her in danger, has maybe exposed whatever it is she is doing. Footsteps approach. Would she be okay? Had he missed some kind of subtext in her poem, which was actually a cry for help?

He meets the owner in the hall. It must have been her footsteps he heard. She looks behind him as she asks if everything is all right and if he would like to join her in the office for a cup of tea. He makes an excuse of not feeling well and thanks her for the tour just as a buzzer announces the end of shift.

By the time he is outside, Wei, his driver, is running to catch up. It's now late in the afternoon. Long shadows dance at the feet of the workers who make their way home. He pushes through the throng toward the parked car. Somebody grabs his arm. Tingles of fear crackle through him, but it's just a young girl with clear brown eyes and black hair pulled into a ponytail. Her daughter, perhaps. She places something in his hand and then merges with the crowd.

Without looking at it, he can tell it's a book. He instinctively stashes it in his coat pocket, taking the place of the poem that he realizes now, in his haste to depart, he has left with the foreman. The message has returned home. He curses softly.

They get in the car, and as they leave, he laughs out loud. Wei looks at him in his rearview mirror, forcing him to turn his head and conceal his smile. The book is heavy in his pocket but is too special to risk looking at now. The trip back to the airport is uneventful, but it is only after his plane takes off that he relaxes. He had watched the face of every passenger who boarded, half expecting they were coming to take his book from him.

The man sitting next to him smells of an aftershave he used to wear when courting his wife. Back then, it was cheap but now is expensive, and he won't spend the money. The man is young and well-dressed, probably only recently graduated to business class. Single, working long hours and assured of his future success in life, unaware yet of how stealthily frustration and disappointment creep up behind, how easy it is to fool oneself about what matters, and how best to spend time.

He waits a while before reaching into his pocket for the book. It's small with a black cover and red spine. He recognizes the paper and her delicate handwriting. Some of the pages have been torn out. Did his poem come from this book? He wonders if he should show it to his children, tell them what little he knows about the people who make their toys. Or is it their right to at least have a childhood free of paradox?

After flipping through the book, he is already planning how to get it translated, eager to read what else she has to say.

He smiles as he puts it away. It's already the most precious book he owns.

\* \* \*

*This story is a part of our legacy-of-excellence program, first printed in the After Dinner Conversation—April 2021 issue.*

# Discussion Questions

1. What do you think the poem means? How much can we tell about the author from it?
2. Do you want to know the conditions/situation of the workers who produce various toys, fruits, or other consumer products you use?
3. Is it fair to be burdened with knowing (*or force other people to know*) the myriad effects of their choices on others?
4. Presumably, the author of the poem (1) lives a somewhat unhappy life and (2) is living the best life possible given her situation. Should the narrator feel guilty for keeping the woman employed through his purchases? What (if anything) should he feel guilty for?
5. What (if anything) should the narrator have done differently in this story and why?

* * *

# Take-em!

## *Charles Williams*

\* \* \*

"Okay Dad, I'll come for the long weekend, but I'm not sure I want to hunt with you," Joey said as he wound up his longest conversation with his father in years. "Those couple of hunts you took me on when I was thirteen didn't make a hunter out of me. I just remember being cold and that we didn't shoot much. Anyway, I don't know that I'm the type to enjoy killing things."

Joey's parents had divorced six years ago, and his mother had moved them to a busy metropolitan area on the east coast. During those years, he'd seen very little of his father whose work as a petroleum engineer required extensive periods of foreign travel and residency. Joey's experiences of nature and wildlife were limited to the local parks of Chevy Chase, Maryland, where hunting was neither encouraged or tolerated, camo clothing was regarded as a symbol of ignorance, and most people didn't know a mallard from a mockingbird. Through deep immersion in urban life, he'd acquired the belief that hunting, for sure, and maybe fishing, too, were at best questionable activities not suited to the modern age of a growing population, environmental problems of all sorts, and scarce resources. But he respected his father as a well-educated man, known as a staunch environmentalist of his community, who had hunted from boyhood on. What was the appeal of it? Why was he still doing it at the age of fifty? Now nineteen and starting his junior year of college, Joey really wanted to reestablish a relationship with his father, man to man, as he envisioned it, and he would explain his reasons for doubt about the proposed hunt, now just a few weeks away. Whether he hunted or not, Joey hoped they would become close again by the experience. And maybe he would even find something positive about hunting if he gave it a chance.

Joey recalled the carefully chosen but blunt words that he'd used to tell his father about his view of sport hunting. "It's immoral," he'd said, "to kill a living creature for recreation, especially when the deck is stacked in your favor with all the modern technology, high-powered weapons and shells, mechanical decoys, and such."

His father had been quick with a response. "Son, the main objective isn't the killing. It's the hunt that men have engaged in for millennia and, until relatively recent times, was the human race's main way of getting food. The rational part of your city boy's brain may not like hunting, but in fact, hunting is embedded in our genes. The chase of game and killing the game, from mastodons to birds, goes back tens of thousands of years and was the most important thing men did, and they had to do it well or die."

The response had not surprised Joey as he had read and

heard that sort of defense of hunting before. He'd answered, "It's no longer necessary to hunt for food, and hunting simply encourages ancient behaviors that should be allowed to die out. Forget the Cro-Magnon stuff!"

His father laughed. "Genetics don't go away that quickly. Maybe if I live another thousand years, I would see some men who've lost the hunting instinct, but for now, we've still got it whether we like it or not—and that includes you, Joey."

Joey had scoffed at that point and then moved to his second point. "Another problem with hunting and fishing is we just don't need to do it. We can get all the healthy food we need right up at the corner grocery store. Why not buy food at the store, skip the hunting, and use the time saved for civilized activities?"

Then it was his father's chance to express skepticism. "Healthy food is a byproduct of hunting. Wild game has better flavor, lower fat content, fewer chemicals, and so forth. And there're lots of other good reasons for hunting besides getting food uncontaminated by modern additives—removal of overpopulated animals as determined by professional game managers, protection of habitat for game that also protects non-game birds and animals, and more people being aware of the outdoors and committed to preserving the environment. Half the birdwatchers I know developed their love of nature and support of wilderness areas in early life hunting and fishing with their fathers. Today's kids just want to play video games, and organizations that help protect the environment are falling apart due to having fewer and fewer people who care. We're losing an entire generation from the experience and love of nature as it really is."

Joey enjoyed the convoluted defense and continued the bantering tone. "Sounds like blood sports propaganda to me. I still say killing animals for fun is just plain wrong no matter how much lipstick you try to put on it. Morally produced and organic products, certified by independent groups testifying to the proper treatment of the animals, are readily available."

"Aw you know that's just a tiny part of what you see in stores. How is a domestic chicken on your plate, a product of a polluting industrial-scale operation, morally superior to a wild duck on that same plate that you shot yourself? And just envision all the air and water pollution that comes from a chicken processing plant. The jobs in that plant are the lowest paying and nastiest in America today. Aren't you just farming out the dirty work of killing the poultry to unskilled workers? Who benefits from that? What is the morality of it? Do it yourself! Come hunting with me!"

Joey reiterated, "I'd just as soon buy a supermarket duck that was treated well, had some open range to run around in, and was dispatched humanely."

"Did you say propaganda a minute ago? For hogs and cows, that open range you mentioned is usually a five-by-five cage instead of the usual three by three. Don't be naïve and think the animals are real happy with that difference."

Joey still didn't buy the idea of hunting. "You never feel bad when you shoot a wild bird? You kill something that's beautiful and free just for a little sport. And what about the ones that're wounded?

Again, his father had an answer. "The birds I shoot have had a great life of living free. Think how much better their life was than your chicken's in his slightly larger cage. And if I cripple a bird, I always hunt it down and give it a quick ending."

"That's anthropomorphic thinking, Dad, and you know it. Neither the duck or the chicken or a deer or whatever has any perception of being free or not free prior to its death. It just exists, then dies. I still say there's no reason to kill a wild duck. You can go out and watch ducks and other birds with just binocs in hand, and you can stop by the store on the way home and buy some organic chicken or beef. So you satisfy both your urge to be in nature and your need for food without firing a shot!"

\* \* \*

Joey and his dad went around and around like this, seemingly in circles, for at least an hour. They got into many side issues of their debate. Did the morality change if the species hunted, location, methods employed, or other factors changed? His dad made the point that deer hunting was absolutely necessary in modern life because mankind had eliminated all the apex predators except himself. Without hunters, deer would overrun the landscape and damage nature for many species of birds and other animals as well as for humans. The discussion was lively and a feeling of respect seemed to grow between them despite the differences.

His father finally implored him. "Let me take you out Saturday morning, two weeks from now, for opening day and let's see if you stick with your idea that sport hunting is wrong."

Joey finally agreed. He felt satisfied with the points against hunting he'd made and was impressed with the logic of his dad's responses, but he was still on the fence about whether he'd actually do any shooting. Maybe he'd just watch.

\* \* \*

Joey and his father were mostly silent on the drive to the

marsh on opening day. Forty-five minutes into the trip, his father pulled the truck off the highway onto a crude gravel road that led past some oil wells to a boat landing, which was just a clearing in the marsh. His father turned off the ignition but didn't open his door. He turned to Joey and asked, "So are we hunting, or are we going to turn around and go back home?"

The clear sky was incredibly dark as there were no buildings or electric lighting anywhere in the area. The stars and constellations seemed as though they were magnified. In Chevy Chase at night, he could only see a few really bright stars and had never had a good look at a constellation. Sunrise was still an hour away, but bird calls of all sorts were starting—his father identified for him the calls of rails, ducks, geese, herons, as well as the yipping of coyotes and the deep croaks of bullfrogs. It was a wondrous moment, and he quickly identified with his father's love of being in nature as sunrise approached. But why did they have to ruin it by bringing guns to kill ducks? As a gesture of companionship and respect for his father, should he join the hunt this once? Was it possible he could conclude that his father was right about blood sports, that what they were about to do was no worse than paying others—butchers, chicken processors, hog slaughterers—to do his dirty work for him? And even in modern times, that human hunters still played an important role in ecological balance?

The boat landing consisted of just a gravel slope leading into the water of a small bayou. There they loaded a john boat with decoys, guns, shells, and a bag with hot chocolate and snacks. They poled the boat a short distance to the beginning of a trenasse that would take them to the pond with his dad's duck blind on its north edge. There they placed the decoys in an arc leaving an open space for landing ducks. His dad explained, "They'll land into this north wind we've got. We'll shoot just as they're hovering over the water." Joey focused on the words "we'll shoot" and wondered. No doubt his dad would shoot, but would he also pull the trigger? Would he, upon seeing the helpless ducks barely moving as they decelerated into the wind before landing, fire his gun? Or would he aim high, deliberately missing? Could he bear the sight of a beautiful wild duck he himself had just killed? He wasn't sure. Even worse, would he just wound a duck and then have to chase it down in the marsh and wring its neck to finish it off? But he kept thinking, trying to will himself to please his dad at the critical moment. An act that could bring them back together, or if not done, might widen the gulf between them.

During the next half hour after putting out the decoys, they sat quietly in the blind as light began to appear slowly on the horizon with the impending sunrise. The silhouettes of flying birds of many kinds could be seen passing in front of the gradually lightening blue, orange, and golden sky to the east. In those minutes, Joey reveled in his first adult experience of the sights and sounds of sunrise on a marsh, and his book learning about nature paled in comparison. Finally, his father announced, "It's shooting time. Next ducks that come in we'll take. Remember, wait till I say "Take 'em" and come up fast. I won't call the shot until they're in good range."

Less than five minutes later, his father whispered, "Mallards coming from two o'clock; they're cupping. Get ready."

Joey looked to the right front of the blind, and just over the tall Roseau cane that defined the opposite shore of the pond, he could see about a dozen ducks, making a beeline for the decoys from a few hundred yards away. Still crouching behind the vegetation at the front of the blind, Joey's left hand trembled as he eased the shotgun up where he could grip it with both hands. He placed his right hand on the stock, his finger ready to release the safety on the trigger guard.

Closer, closer... his focus intense and his hands shaking a little, he lost all consciousness of questions of the morality of what he was doing. He was completely absorbed in the primordial chase, approaching the climactic moment of completing an ancient ritual—yes, it was the kill. His dad gave a few soft quacks on a call, and the birds wheeled left, pitching perfectly into the middle of the decoys, an easy shot as his dad had predicted. Then his dad gave the command, "Take 'em!" Joey threw his gun to his shoulder, swung the shotgun on a flaring drake mallard, and pulled the trigger.

* * *

*This story is a part of our legacy-of-excellence program, first printed in the After Dinner Conversation—April 2021 issue.*

# Discussion Questions

1. It's clear Joey's Dad knows Joey doesn't want to shoot ducks; is it wrong of the father to ask him to do it? Does Joey's father know he is leveraging his emotional connection to cause his son pain for his own personal satisfaction? Would it matter if he did know?

2. How do you know when you are having a lively debate on the merits versus pressuring someone into doing something against their preferences? Should a conversation simply stop after the first person says, "no thank you"?

3. What is the strongest argument Joey makes against hunting? What is the strongest argument his father makes in support of hunting?

4. Is the situation in the story different than someone being coerced into having sex from someone whom they want approval? What makes it different (*or not different*)?

5. Is there a variation of this story where Joey should simply "go along?" What is a variation where he should say no? What is the ideological distinction between the two variations?

\* \* \*

# <u>Author Information</u>

### <u>Being Wrong</u>

**Lise Halpern** has turned her thousand word a day writing habit to more literary pursuits after decades of writing the creative fiction in the form of strategic business plans and advertising copy. She resides with two crazy border collies in a river town in bucolic Bucks County, Pennsylvania. *www.lisehalpern.com*

### <u>The Children of Conscious Reunion</u>

**M.C. Schmidt's** recent short fiction has appeared in EVENT, Spectrum Literary Journal, Prose Online, Eclectica, X-R-A-Y, and elsewhere. He is the author of the novel, *The Decadents* (Library Tales Publishing, 2022). He holds an MFA in Creative Writing from Miami University.

### <u>The Pill</u>

**Thea Swanson** is a feminist atheist who holds an MFA in Writing from Pacific University in Oregon. She is the Founding Editor of *Club Plum Literary Journal*, and her dystopian flash-fiction collection, *Mars*, was published by Ravenna Press in 2017. She is a pushcart prize nominee and is published in places such as *Chicago Review of Books*, *World Literature Today, Mid-American Review* and elsewhere. X (Twitter) *@thea_swanson*; Instagram *@swanson.thea*; *www.theaswanson.com*.

### <u>Yellow Is the Color of Choices</u>

**Penny Milam** has taught high-school English for many years. Her work has appeared in Valparaiso Fiction Review, Variant Literature, and Hypertext, among others. She lives in East Tennessee with her husband and three children. Instagram *@milam.penny*; *www.pennyapple.net*

## Whose Life Is It

**Deborah Serra** is a double recipient of the Hawthornden Literary Fellowship. Her first novel was a semi-finalist for the Faulkner-Wisdom Creative Writing Award. On assignment, she has written ten TV films. She has written three award-winning plays and has been published by several literary journals. She has taught at UCSD and is a sought-after creative editor for fiction and non-fiction. Member of WGA, DG, PEN USA. *www.deborahserra.com*

## Reach

**Mark Braidwood** is a medical doctor and writes part-time. His short story "The Auction" was published in the Aurora-winning *Polar Borealis* and selected for the "Stellar Evolutions, Best of Fifteen" anthology. His short story "Coincidence" was a finalist in the *Writers of the Future* competition and his first novel was shortlisted in the *Fantastica* science fiction prize. He has also contributed to a book about climate change and health.

## Take-em!

**Charles Williams** a native of Louisiana, retired from a career in real estate finance and took up writing fiction as a retirement avocation. He writes stories emphasizing Louisiana settings, themes, and characters. Charles resided in New Orleans for ten years and currently resides in Baton Rouge. He has a B.A. from Centenary College, an M.A. from LSU, and an MBA from The Wharton School.

# Additional Information

## Reviews

If you enjoyed reading these stories, please consider doing an online review. It's only a few seconds of your time, but it is very important in continuing the series. Good reviews mean higher rankings. Higher rankings mean more sales and a greater ability to release stories.

## Print Anthology Series

*https://www.afterdinnerconversation.com*

Purchase our growing collection of print anthologies. They are collections of our best short stories published in the After Dinner Conversation series, complete with discussion questions.

## Podcast Discussions/Audiobooks

*https://www.afterdinnerconversation.com/podcastlinks*

Listen to our podcast discussions and audiobooks of After Dinner Conversation short stories on Apple, Spotify, or wherever podcasts are played. Or, if you prefer, watch the podcasts on our YouTube channel or download the .mp3 file directly from our website.

## Patreon

*https://www.patreon.com/afterdinnerconversation*

Get early access to short stories and ad-free podcasts. New supporters also get a free digital copy of the anthology *After Dinner Conversation– Season One*. Support us on Patreon!

## Book Clubs/Classrooms

*https://www.afterdinnerconversation.com/book-club-downloads*

After Dinner Conversation supports book clubs! Receive free short stories for your book club to read and discuss!

## Social

Connect with us on Facebook, YouTube, Instagram, TikTok, Substack, and X (Twitter).

Printed in Great Britain
by Amazon

32304658R00057